वक्रतुंड महाकाय सूर्यकोटिसमप्रभ ।
निर्विघ्नं कुरु मे देव सर्वकार्येषु सर्वदा ॥

The Billionaire Mystic

How Tarot and Tenacity Transformed a Woman's Life

Author - Shalini Pathak

Content

Dedication

To every soul seeking more—more success, more meaning, more balance, and more light.

This book is for you who dream of material prosperity while longing for spiritual peace, for those yearning to improve their lives in any way, be it wealth, emotional health, or a deeper sense of purpose.

To those who feel stuck, unsure of the path ahead, and crave the gentle nudge of direction toward a brighter, more aligned future.

To everyone seeking harmony between ambition and inner tranquillity, striving to connect with their higher self while achieving fulfilment in the physical world.

May this book guide you to unlock the immense potential within, to balance your heart with your mind, and your spirit with your goals. May it inspire you to align with the abundant energy of the universe and find joy in every step of your journey.

This is for you, dear reader, as you create a life of both extraordinary success and profound satisfaction.

With love and light,
Shalini Pathak

Acknowledgments

With a heart full of gratitude, I offer my deepest thanks to the divine powers that have guided me throughout this journey:

Gurudev Neem Karori Baba: For illuminating my path with wisdom and showing me the way when all seemed dark. For being a spiritual beacon, radiating simplicity and grace, and teaching the power of surrender and faith.

गुरू ब्रह्मा गुरू विष्णु, गुरु देवो महेश्वरा गुरु साक्षात परब्रह्म, तस्मै श्री गुरुवे नम:

Guru (the teacher) is Brahma (the force of creation); Guru is Vishnu (the force of preservation), Guru is Maheshwara (the force of destruction and transformation), Guru is the embodiment of Para Brahma, the ultimate Godhead. We bow down to that Guru.

Hanuman Ji: For being the epitome of strength, devotion, and self-realization. Your unwavering energy inspires me to face life's challenges with courage.

मनोजवं मारुततुल्यवेगं जितेन्द्रियं बुद्धिमतां वरिष्ठम्।
वातात्मजं वानरयूथमुख्यं श्रीरामदूतम् शरणं प्रपद्ये।।

Who is Swift as Mind and Fast as Wind, Who is the Master of the Senses and Honoured for His Excellent Intelligence, Learning and Wisdom, Who is Son of the Wind God and Chief among the Monkeys, To that Messenger of Sri Rama, I take Refuge.

Lord Ram: For teaching me the value of righteousness, compassion, and perseverance.

नीलाम्बुजश्यामलकोमलाङ्गं सीतासमारोपितवामभागम।
पाणौ महासायकचारूचापं, नमामि रामं रघुवंशनाथम॥

Whose body has the colour of a blue lotus and grey, whose body parts are soft, on whose left side resides Sita Who has a transcendental arrow and a beautiful bow in His hands I pray to that Sri Ram who is the Lord of Raghu dynasty.

Your blessings have been the foundation of this book and my life. Thank you for the endless love, guidance, and miracles.

Preface

The Billionaire Mystic is not just a story; it is a journey—a pathway to discovering the infinite potential that lies within each of us. In today's world, where the race for material success often leaves our spirits yearning for meaning, this book seeks to bridge the gap between two seemingly opposite realms: the materialistic and the spiritual.

As you follow the extraordinary tale of Aurora—a woman who rose from adversity to triumph in the business world while embarking on a spiritual quest—you will see yourself mirrored in her struggles, her aspirations, and her transformation. Aurora's journey is not merely fictional; it is a reflection of the battles we all fight within ourselves, the choices we make, and the power we hold to shape our destiny.

Through this book, I, Shalini Pathak, share not only Aurora's inspiring story but also the timeless wisdom rooted in ancient Indian mythology and modern strategies for success. As someone deeply immersed in astrology, meditation, and spiritual healing, my mission is to guide others to realize that the divine resides within them. The secrets to achieving material abundance and spiritual enlightenment are not distant goals but interconnected facets of the same human potential.

The Billionaire Mystic aims to awaken that potential within you. It serves as a reminder that every setback is a setup for a comeback and that true fulfillment lies in mastering both the outer world of achievements and the inner world of peace and wisdom.

May this book inspire you to embrace your journey with courage and purpose, to conquer your fears, and to manifest the life you were always meant to live.

With gratitude and love,
Shalini Pathak
Astrologer, Healer, and Life Coach

Prologue

In a world where success is often measured by material achievements, the essence of the soul is sometimes forgotten. Yet, deep within, there exists an untapped reservoir of divine potential—waiting to be awakened. *The Billionaire Mystic* is a story, a guide, and a reminder that true success lies in mastering both realms: the material and the spiritual.

Aurora's journey mirrors the struggles and triumphs we all face—a quest for love, belonging, and purpose. But her ultimate realization is one that resonates universally: all the power to transform your life lies within.

Through this narrative, coupled with lessons from timeless scriptures like the *Hanuman Chalisa* and *Sunderkand*, you'll discover that the universe is always conspiring in your favor. The only question is, are you ready to rise?

"Life completes its circle in the harmony of opposites—dark and light, up and down, earth and sky, left and right, silence and music—each contrast weaving the symphony of existence."

Epigraph

"Within you lies the infinite—wealth and wisdom, strength and surrender. To master life is to align with the divine rhythm, where the material and spiritual dance as one."

"Whatever you seek is already within you. It is only by turning inward that you can change the world outward."

Author Introduction

Shalini Pathak "Student by Heart", the author of *The Billionaire Mystic*, is a renowned astrologer, healer, and life coach with over 16 years of experience in life management and personal transformation. With an exceptional ability to blend spiritual wisdom with practical strategies, she has guided countless individuals toward achieving success in both their material and spiritual lives.

Shalini's journey is as inspiring as the stories she shares. Having worked with several private companies before establishing her own firm, *Divine Guidance*, she brings a unique perspective to life's challenges. Her company specializes in astrology, healing, and coaching, offering personalized strategies that empower individuals to overcome obstacles, harness their inner potential, and create winning outcomes in life.

Deeply rooted in meditation and the ancient teachings of Indian mythology and scriptures, Shalini combines timeless spiritual principles with actionable insights. Her approach resonates with people from all walks of life, encouraging them to unlock the divine abilities that lie dormant within them and to strive for greatness in all aspects of existence.

Through *The Billionaire Mystic*, Shalini shares her vision of a balanced life—where material success complements spiritual growth. This book is her heartfelt endeavor to inspire readers to master their potential, rise above challenges, and embrace the extraordinary within.

When she's not writing or coaching, Shalini dedicates her time to meditation, self-discovery, and deepening her understanding of ancient wisdom. Her passion for uplifting others and her transformative insights make her a guiding light for those seeking purpose, success, and fulfillment.

"Surrender to a true Guru is not submission, but the opening of your soul to divine wisdom and limitless growth."

Thank You Note

First and foremost, I extend my heartfelt gratitude to the Universe for guiding me throughout this incredible journey. Every step, every challenge, and every revelation has been divinely orchestrated, leading me to this moment where *The Billionaire Mystic* comes to life. Thank you for the inspiration, clarity, and strength to transform my vision into reality.

To my family, your unwavering support has been my anchor and my motivation. Thank you for believing in me and for standing by my side as I poured my heart and soul into this book. Each of you has contributed in your unique way, helping me weave my story and share it with the world.

A very special thank you to my best friend Akshay and younger sister, Shivani, for her creative brilliance and endless encouragement. Shivani, your vision for the cover and title of this book has brought my work to life in the most beautiful way. Your dedication and talent are a gift, and I am forever grateful for your invaluable contribution.

To everyone who has shared their insights, connected the dots in my journey, and encouraged me to keep moving forward—you are all part of this book's soul. Thank you for your love, your belief in my dreams, and your faith in the message this book carries.

**With love and gratitude,
Shalini Pathak**

Chapter One: A Gift from the Universe

Aurora's earliest memories were a delicate balance of love and hardship. She remembered Clara's lullabies, hummed softly in the dim light of their small house. Though her voice sometimes trembled with exhaustion, those melodies wrapped Aurora in a fragile cocoon of safety. Victor, with his large, calloused hands, would fix broken furniture around the house, his focus intense as though he could mend their fractured lives.

Their love was evident in small gestures—Clara tucking Aurora into bed with whispered promises, and Victor teaching her to draw on scraps of paper, guiding her hand with surprising tenderness. Yet, beneath these tender moments, a shadow of past loomed.

In Clara's thought when they were gifted by mother nature, in the quiet village of **Verdalia**, nestled amidst endless fields of golden wheat and verdant forests, life moved at a slow and predictable pace. Verdalia was untouched by modern technology, where people lived in harmony with nature, relying on the land and the seasons for their needs.

Clara and Victor were among the hardworking villagers, a humble couple who worked tirelessly in the fields of a wealthy landlord to earn their daily wages. They lived simply but were known for their kindness, integrity, and deep love for each other.

One serene morning, as Clara and Victor walked through the village's tranquil garden on their way to the landlord's fields, a sight stopped them in their tracks. Amidst the soft green grass, beneath the dappled sunlight filtering through the trees, lay a baby girl no older than three months. She wasn't crying but instead cooing softly, her tiny fingers clutching at a strand of grass as if she belonged perfectly to the earth around her.

Clara gasped, clutching Victor's arm. "Victor, look... a baby. Where could she have come from?"

Victor's eyes were wide with awe. "She's glowing," he whispered, his voice filled with wonder.

They moved closer, their steps hesitant but drawn by an unspoken pull. As they reached her, they noticed a small shining crystal hanging from her neck, tied with a white-golden thread that shimmered in the sunlight. The baby radiated a sense of peace and purity, her presence almost otherworldly.

Beside her lay a deck of Tarot cards, intricately designed with symbols that neither of them recognized, their edges glimmering faintly. Clara knelt down and gently picked up the baby, cradling her close. The little girl's laughter bubbled up, filling the air with warmth.

Victor picked up the Tarot deck, turning it over in his hands, and glanced at the crystal locket she wore. "Whoever left her here... they must have wanted her to be found. She's no ordinary child, Clara."

Clara's eyes filled with tears as she looked at the baby in her arms. "Maybe she was meant to find us, Victor. Maybe she's our blessing."

Victor nodded, his heart swelling with a mix of joy and responsibility. They didn't question further. Instead, they embraced the moment, accepting the baby girl as their own.

From that day forward, the garden became more than a pathway to the fields—it became the sacred place where their family began, bound by a love that would transcend their understanding of destiny.

Clara gasped, her eyes darting between the baby and the tarot deck. "Victor... this is no coincidence. She's special. She was sent to us."

"She's a gift," Victor said, his voice heavy with emotion. "From mother nature herself. And these Tarot Cards... it must be part of her destiny."

Clara nodded, tears streaming down her cheeks. "Then we'll protect her, love her, and raise her as our own."

From that moment on, their lives changed forever. They named the child **Aurora**, inspired by the radiant light they had seen around her that morning. The Tarot deck, placed safely in their home, kept as sacred items, though they never truly understood their purpose.

Aurora grew up in Clara and Victor's modest home—a simple clay house with a thatched roof and a warm hearth. Despite their humble means, Clara and Victor raised her with immense love and care, teaching her the values of kindness, hard work, and gratitude.

The Tarot deck remained untouched for years. Clara often glanced at them, feeling a strange reverence, but neither she nor Victor ever dared to use or move them unnecessarily.

Aurora was an extraordinary child. By the time she was five, she had begun helping Clara with chores and assisting Victor in the fields. She had an innate curiosity about the world and excelled at the village school, a one-room building where children of all ages learned together.

Her quick intelligence and gentle nature earned her the admiration of her peers, though she preferred to keep to herself. Many children wanted to be her friends, but Aurora hesitated to let anyone get too close—except for **Elias**, her best friend.

Elias was a cheerful and loyal boy who lived nearby. The two were inseparable, sharing their dreams and secrets under the shade of Verdalia's ancient banyan tree.

Though Aurora never touched the Tarot deck she often felt its presence in her home, as if its quietly calling to her. Sometimes, in moments of stillness, she would stare at the bag, a strange sense of familiarity washing over her.

One evening, as Aurora sat by the hearth, the soft crackle of the fire soothing her after a long day, her gaze fell upon a small, intricately crafted bag resting on the mantel. Its design seemed otherworldly, with shimmering threads that caught the light in mesmerizing patterns.

"Mama," Aurora said, her voice tinged with curiosity, "where did that bag come from?"

Clara looked up from her knitting, a gentle smile spreading across her face. She set her work aside and moved to sit beside Aurora, brushing a strand of hair from her daughter's face. "We found it as a gift for you," she said warmly, her tone carrying a hint of mystery. "A friend of ours gave it to us long ago and told us it was meant for you."

Aurora's brow furrowed slightly. "Why haven't I seen it before? Why didn't we use it?"

Victor, sitting across the room with a book in hand, glanced up and added with a thoughtful smile, "Because it wasn't ours to use, Aurora. We always knew it held a special purpose—one that only you would understand when the time came."

Aurora picked up the bag, her fingers tracing the intricate patterns. Though she didn't fully grasp its significance, she felt a strange connection to it, as if it were a part of her destiny waiting to unfold. "It feels… alive," she whispered, her voice laced with wonder.

Clara nodded knowingly, her eyes glistening with emotion. "It is meant to be yours, my dear. You'll understand its purpose when the moment is right."

Years passed, and the items remained untouched. But one day, something within Aurora stirred—a quiet, insistent pull. She felt ready to open the bag, to see what it held for her, and to discover the path it was meant to illuminate. That day, her journey would truly begin.

Six years old, Aurora had blossomed into a remarkable child, her brilliance shining like the sun over their modest village of **Verdalia**. Her curious mind, quick grasp of knowledge, and intuitive nature made her stand out even in a village where education was scarce and life revolved around simplicity.

Aurora excelled in her studies at the local school, where she eagerly absorbed everything her teacher taught. Whether it was reading, arithmetic, or reciting poems, she had a knack for mastering concepts swiftly. Her teacher often remarked to Clara and Victor, "She's a little star. There's a wisdom in her that I cannot quite explain."

But Aurora's talents weren't limited to academics. Music and art came to her as naturally as breathing. She loved crafting melodies on the village's only old harmonium, gifted by a retired musician. The tunes she played were simple but hauntingly beautiful, evoking a sense of peace and wonder in anyone who listened. Her artwork, made from whatever scraps and colors she could find, captured the essence of Verdalia's natural beauty—the rivers, the fields, the towering trees, and the luminous sky.

Her connection to nature was unparalleled. Aurora would spend hours exploring the woods, observing every leaf, every fluttering butterfly, and every rustling of the trees as if she understood their language. Clara often joked that the birds sang louder when Aurora was near, as though they recognized one of their own.

One of Aurora's favorite moments was the evenings she spent with Clara, Victor, or Elias beneath the starlit sky. Clara, with her soothing voice, would weave enchanting tales of mythical heroes and heroines—stories of courage, kindness, and the eternal triumph of good over evil.

Aurora's eyes sparkled with wonder as Clara described battles fought by ancient warriors wielding swords of light, queens who protected their realms with wisdom, and magical beings who bridged the worlds of mortals and gods. Clara would always end her stories with a gentle reminder, "No matter how strong the darkness, it will always yield to the light, my child. Never forget that." Aurora never did.

She would gaze at the stars, connecting the characters and events Clara spoke of to the constellations above. She imagined the stars as guardians of the universe, winking down at her in silent reassurance that goodness was always watching.

Her best friend Elias often joined them, listening intently or pointing out stars and shapes in the sky. Though Aurora was reserved with most children, Elias was her confidant. She trusted him with her thoughts and dreams, and he, in turn, admired her like one might admire a rare treasure.

Aurora's bond with Clara was unbreakable. Like a shadow, she followed Clara everywhere—from the kitchen where Clara kneaded dough and prepared humble meals, to the fields where she worked tirelessly under the sun. Aurora insisted on helping with whatever task Clara took on, no matter how small. She would gather firewood, fetch water, or hold the basket as Clara harvested vegetables.

During their shared moments of prayer, Aurora mirrored Clara with unwavering focus. Together, they knelt before the small wooden shrine in their home, adorned with a few candles and a picture of a deity, whispering prayers of gratitude and protection. Aurora's voice was soft but steady, filled with an earnestness that belied her age.

Clara often marveled at her daughter's maturity and intuition. There were times when Aurora would say something so profound, it left Clara speechless. Once, while watching the sun set over the hills, Aurora had remarked, "The sun never disappears, Mama. It just moves to give the moon its turn to shine. Maybe we're like that too—helping each other take turns to glow."

Clara smiled, brushing a stray lock of hair from Aurora's face. "You're wise beyond your years, my little one," she said, planting a kiss on her forehead.

Aurora's imagination knew no bounds. Every rustle of the wind, every ripple in the stream, and every shadow cast by the trees became part of her stories. She would create entire worlds in her mind, often narrating them to Elias or sketching them on scraps of paper.

Her intuition, too, grew stronger with each passing day. Aurora seemed to sense things before they happened—a sudden change in the weather, the arrival of a visitor, or the mood of the people around her. Clara noticed how Aurora's presence had a calming effect on animals, from the village cows to the stray dogs that roamed the streets.

"She's special, Victor," Clara would often say to her husband. "There's a light in her that the world hasn't yet seen."

Victor, though a man of few words, nodded in agreement. "She's our blessing. A gift from the stars."

Though Aurora didn't yet understand the full extent of her uniqueness, her actions hinted at a destiny far greater than the simple life she led in Verdalia. With every task she undertook, every melody she played, and every story she absorbed, she was preparing—unknowingly—for a path that would one day lead her to her true purpose.

Her best friend, Elias, was her only tether to joy. With his sandy hair and infectious grin, he brought light into her often somber life. They spent countless hours at the park, dreaming of adventures and a world beyond the city's gray confines.

Aurora's life in Verdalia was filled with warmth, simplicity, and the bond she shared with Clara and Victor. But one fateful day, that sense of security was shaken. Her best friend, Elias, disappeared without a trace.

It happened without warning. One moment, he was playing by the river, his laughter mingling with the soft rustling of the trees. The next, he was gone. The villagers searched every nook and corner of the surrounding forests and fields, calling his name until their voices cracked, but there was no sign of him.

Aurora was inconsolable. She clung to Clara's skirt, her small fists trembling as tears streamed down her face.

"Where has Elias gone, Mama? When will he come back? Why did he leave me?"

Clara knelt to Aurora's level, her heart breaking at the sight of her grief. She pulled her into a tight embrace and stroked her hair gently.

"Sometimes, people leave us without any reason, my love," she whispered, her voice heavy with sorrow. *"We don't always understand why, but we must keep them in our hearts and hope they find their way."*

Aurora cried herself to sleep that night, clutching the small wooden toy Elias had gifted her on her last birthday. Each day that followed, she would look toward the horizon, hoping to see her friend running back to her with his familiar grin. But days turned into weeks, and weeks into years. The emptiness Elias left behind became a quiet ache that Aurora carried with her, hidden beneath her radiant smile.

Chapter -2: The Secret of Her Origins

By the time Aurora turned sixteen, she had grown into a curious, intelligent, and compassionate young girl. Her teachers continued to marvel at her brilliance, and her bond with Clara and Victor remained as strong as ever. Yet, there was a quiet restlessness in her heart—a yearning she couldn't quite explain.

One evening, as Aurora lay in bed, the murmured voices of Clara and Victor floated through the thin walls of their small home, mingling with the gentle crackle of the hearth in the kitchen.

"She deserves so much more, Victor," Clara said, her voice resolute yet tinged with longing. "Aurora is meant for greater things than this village. We need to save every penny we can to send her to the city for her studies. She should learn about computers, modern science, and everything that can give her a brighter future. She shouldn't spend her life toiling in the fields like we do."

Victor let out a weary sigh, his voice heavy with a mix of agreement and worry. "You're right, Clara. She's destined for something bigger. But..." He hesitated, the weight of his thoughts pressing on him. "What if one day someone comes looking for her? Her relatives, her parents? What will we say if they demand to take her back? What will we tell her if she asks where she truly comes from?"

Clara's voice softened, filled with emotion. "She may not be ours by blood, Victor, but she is our daughter in every way that matters. Mother Nature brought her to us for a reason. We've loved her, nurtured her, and watched her grow. If anyone comes... we'll cross that bridge when we get there. For now, all that matters is giving her the future she deserves."

Victor nodded, though the unease lingered in his heart. Together, they silently vowed to do whatever it took to secure a better life for Aurora, even as questions about her past loomed in the shadows.

Aurora's breath caught in her throat. She sat up in bed, her heart pounding. *Not theirs?* The words echoed in her mind, unraveling the foundation of everything she had believed about herself.

The next morning, Aurora confronted Clara. "Mama, what did you mean when you said I'm not yours?"

Clara froze, her eyes wide with shock and guilt. She took a deep breath, kneeling before Aurora and taking her hands in her own. "Aurora, my love, there's something we never told you because we didn't want you to feel different or unloved."

And so, Clara told Aurora the truth about the day they found her—a glowing infant in the garden, wrapped in light, with a mysterious bag containing the Tarot deck. She explained how they had taken her in, believing her to be a gift from Mother Nature, and how they had loved her as their own from that moment on.

"You may not have come from me," Clara said, tears brimming in her eyes, "but you are our daughter in every way that counts. And we will do everything we can to help you grow into the extraordinary person you're meant to be."

Victor stepped in, placing a gentle hand on Aurora's shoulder. "We love you, Aurora. That will never change."

Though the revelation left Aurora with more questions than answers, it also filled her with a sense of purpose. If she wasn't born to Clara and Victor, then where had she come from? Who were her real parents, and why had they left her?

Yet, amidst the swirling uncertainty, one thing remained clear—Clara and Victor were her family. Their love and sacrifices had shaped her into who she was, and she would honor them by embracing every opportunity they worked so hard to give her.

That evening, as Aurora gazed at the stars with Clara, she made a silent vow. She would uncover the truth of her origins when the time was right, but for now, she would focus on making Clara and Victor proud. She would carry their love and lessons with her, just as she carried the memory of Elias, waiting for the day when the universe would reveal the next step in her journey.

Aurora woke up to the soft light of dawn streaming through the window. The birds outside were chirping their usual melodies, but something felt amiss. The small house was eerily quiet. Usually, the comforting sounds of Clara bustling in the kitchen or Victor humming a tune as he prepared for the day would greet her.

"Mom? Dad?" Aurora called out, her voice echoing through the empty house. She searched every corner, her heart pounding louder with each passing second. Their belongings were still there, their beds unmade as though they had simply stepped out—but there was no sign of them.

The night before, everything had been normal. They had shared a simple dinner together, and Clara had spoken at length about life, love, and dreams.

"You know, Aurora," Clara had said, her eyes soft with nostalgia, "I once dreamed of being a singer. I wanted to travel the world, sharing my voice with people everywhere. But then I met Victor, and everything changed. I fell in love so deeply that nothing else mattered. Life took a different turn, but I have no regrets. Love has its way of showing you what truly matters."

Aurora had smiled, resting her head on Clara's lap as they sat under the stars. That memory, so vivid and warm, now felt like a cruel reminder of what she had lost.

She waited all day, hoping they would return. But as the hours stretched into the evening, panic began to set in.

News of Clara and Victor's disappearance spread like wildfire through Verdalia. The villagers gathered, their faces shadowed with suspicion and fear. Whispers turned into accusations, and soon the entire village had turned against Aurora.

"She's cursed," one of the elders declared, *his voice trembling with anger. "First Elias, and now Clara and Victor. This child brings misfortune wherever she goes!"*

Another villager stepped forward, his face twisted with fury. "We've let this outsider stay among us for too long! Nature itself is punishing us for harboring her. It's time we rid ourselves of this curse."

Aurora stood frozen, tears streaming down her face as the villagers stormed into her house. They threw her belongings into the street—her books, the clothes Clara had lovingly stitched for her, and even the mysterious bag with the Tarot deck and crystals. They piled everything together and set it ablaze.

The flames roared, consuming her last ties to the life she had known.

"Leave!" a woman shouted, pointing a shaking finger at Aurora. "You've brought nothing but despair to this village. If you stay, more of us will suffer!"

Aurora fell to her knees, sobbing uncontrollably. "Please, I've done nothing wrong! Clara and Victor loved me—they wouldn't want this!"

But her pleas fell on deaf ears. One by one, the villagers turned their backs on her, their expressions cold and unforgiving.

Under the weight of their hatred and blame, Aurora gathered the few items she could salvage—the Tarot deck and crystals that had miraculously escaped the flames— and left the only home she had ever known.

As she walked down the dirt path leading out of the village, the sun dipped below the horizon, casting long shadows over the fields. The pain of betrayal and loss was a heavy burden, but beneath it all, a spark of resolve began to take shape.

She turned one last time to look at the village, her heart aching for the life she had lost. "I will find out the truth," she whispered to herself. "About Clara and Victor, about Elias, and about who I really am. And I will prove that I'm not a curse."

With nothing but her wits, her courage, and the mysterious Tarot deck to guide her, Aurora set off into the unknown, determined to uncover the secrets of her past and carve out a future that no one could take from her.

After being exiled, Aurora found herself wandering aimlessly until her feet brought her to the village garden, a place that had once been her sanctuary. She sat on the damp grass under the canopy of stars, clutching her knees to her chest. The cool night air stung her tear-soaked cheeks as her mind replayed every moment with Clara and Victor.

"What if they come back?" she whispered to the wind, her voice trembling. "What if they find the house and I'm not there? What if they're looking for me right now?"

The garden was silent except for the rustling of leaves in the breeze. Aurora's heart ached with the hope that was slowly slipping away. She imagined Clara's warm embrace, Victor's reassuring smile, the two of them calling her name and fighting for her against the angry villagers.

But the night stretched on, and no one came.

Her tears dried as hopelessness settled in. The stars above twinkled faintly, as if mocking her loneliness. By dawn, she was shivering—not just from the cold but from the stark realization that no one was coming to save her.

"I can't stay here," she thought, her voice firm despite the quivering of her lips. "I have to leave. I'll go to Luminara. Clara and Victor always said the city held opportunities. Maybe... maybe I'll find something there."

With the little money Victor had saved for her studies and a hard bag that once belonged to Clara, Aurora packed the essentials: a few clothes, her school bag, and the Tarot deck. Her fingers lingered on the bag as she remembered Victor's loving words about her future.

"You'll go to school in the city one day," he had said. "You'll learn everything we never could, and you'll make a life for yourself."

His dream for her felt like a faint light in her dark world now.

Aurora walked to the village bus stop with heavy steps. The villagers turned away as she passed, their faces cold and indifferent. She didn't look back.

The bus ride to Luminara was long, the rumble of the engine a dull backdrop to her racing thoughts. She stared out the window as fields and hills gave way to the sprawling cityscape. Her chest tightened with every mile closer to the unknown.

When she finally stepped off the bus, the city overwhelmed her senses. The air buzzed with the hum of vehicles and chatter. Buildings stretched high into the sky, casting long shadows over the streets. Faces passed by in a blur—rushing, indifferent, and unfamiliar.

Aurora clutched her bags tightly, standing frozen on the crowded platform. For the first time, the reality of her situation hit her.

With no home, no plan, and no one to turn to, Aurora wandered the bus station aimlessly. She sat on an iron bench, her hard bag beside her, and stared blankly at the endless stream of people.

Tears streamed down her face as she whispered prayers to the stars. "Clara, Victor, wherever you are, please come back to me. I'm scared. I don't know what to do. Please, I need you."

Her stomach growled, but she ignored it. The grief was louder than her hunger. She had no appetite, no energy, no will to move.

As night fell, the station lights cast eerie shadows over the deserted benches. Aurora huddled on the iron table, her body trembling with fever and exhaustion. She pressed her palms together and prayed once more, tears wetting her cheeks.

"They won't know I'm here," she murmured through chattering teeth. *"Even if they come back, they won't find me. Maybe I should go back to the village. Maybe the villagers will understand..."*

But she knew the truth. The village had rejected her. There was no place for her there.

The night dragged on, and Aurora's mind swirled with confusion, grief, and fear. Her head throbbed, and her body ached. Fever consumed her, but she couldn't bring herself to sleep. Her heart was too heavy, and her thoughts too loud.

The stars above flickered faintly through the city haze. Aurora stared up at them, her vision blurred with tears. "Why?" she whispered. "Why did this happen to me?"

As the first rays of dawn lit the horizon, Aurora sat motionless, her spirit battered but not broken. She didn't know what the future held, but one thought kept echoing in her mind: *I have to survive.*

Aurora's head throbbed as she wandered the streets in the dim light of early morning. Her body felt weak, her fever intensifying with every passing moment. She desperately needed water, food, and some rest, but the streets were silent, and the small shops she came across were still closed. She sat down on a cold bench near a shuttered storefront, clutching her belongings tightly. She glanced at the horizon, silently pleading for the morning to bring some relief.

After what felt like an eternity, the shops began to open. Aurora spotted a small tea stall with a man arranging cups and cleaning his workspace. Gathering her remaining strength, she approached him and asked for a bottle of water. Her voice was hoarse, her words heavy with exhaustion. The shopkeeper, a simple, middle-aged man with kind eyes, handed her a bottle. She drank greedily, feeling the water soothe her parched throat.

"Can you make me a coffee?" she asked softly, her trembling hands gripping the bottle. "I haven't eaten in... I don't even know how long."

The shopkeeper nodded and prepared a steaming cup of coffee. As Aurora sipped it, she felt a flicker of warmth return to her. Gathering her courage, she hesitated before speaking again.

"I... I need a place to stay," she began, her voice breaking. "I don't have anyone here. I can work. I'll do anything— cleaning, teaching, running errands. I've completed my higher secondary education... but I have no money."

The shopkeeper looked at her thoughtfully, sensing her desperation. After a pause, he said, "I live with my wife and two kids in a small room behind the shop. It's cramped, but if you need a place for a few days, you're welcome to stay with us. You can help with the shop and the house until you find something more permanent."

Aurora's eyes filled with tears. *"Thank you,"* she whispered. *"I'll do my best. I'll clean, I'll cook, I'll help teach your kids—whatever you need."*

The man nodded. "Come, I'll take you there."

He led her to a modest, single-room dwelling behind his shop. His wife, a kind but weary woman, welcomed Aurora with quiet understanding, while their two small children curiously eyed the newcomer. Aurora felt a wave of relief wash over her, though the sadness of her situation still lingered heavily.

Over the next week, Aurora immersed herself in helping the family. She cleaned the shop every morning, served tea and coffee to customers, and helped the children with their studies. Though the work was exhausting, it gave her a sense of purpose and a temporary reprieve from her grief. In return, the family provided her with meals and a corner to sleep in their humble home.

Despite the hardship, Aurora remained determined. She planned to save every rupee she earned to secure a room of her own. The shopkeeper, moved by her resilience, often encouraged her with kind words. "You're strong for someone so young," he told her one evening. "You'll find your way. Just don't lose hope."

Aurora nodded, clutching the golden thread from her Tarot bag for comfort. As she lay down that night, she whispered to the stars, "Clara, Victor... I'm trying to be strong. Please, wherever you are, guide me." Tears slid down her cheeks, but for the first time in days, she felt the faintest glimmer of hope.

Aurora's life continued to take one small step forward amidst the shadow of her overwhelming grief. The shopkeeper, now revealed as "Raghav," helped her secure a modest room to rent not far from his shop. It wasn't much—just a small, bare room with a single cot and a shared bathroom—but to Aurora, it was a place where she could start rebuilding her life.

Before she moved out of Raghav's family home, Aurora stood before them with tears in her eyes.

"Mr. Raghav and Ma'am, you've given me a chance to stand on my own when I had nowhere to go. I owe you everything. I may not have much now, but I promise—if you or your family ever need anything, I'll be there for you. Always," she said earnestly.

Raghav's wife Devi smiled softly. "Take care of yourself, beta. And don't hesitate to visit us. This may be a small city, but good people should stay close."

Aurora nodded, her heart heavy yet grateful, and moved into her new place. She continued working at Raghav's shop for a meager income, just enough to cover her rent and daily meals. Though the days passed, she carried a profound loneliness within her. Memories of Clara and Victor haunted her, and at night, her small room seemed to amplify the silence that surrounded her.

One evening, after a particularly exhausting day at the shop, Aurora felt an unbearable heaviness in her chest. She needed fresh air, a moment away from the suffocating loneliness of her rented room. She grabbed her shawl and walked to a nearby park. The city noise dimmed as she entered the green space, but the ache in her heart only grew stronger.

Sitting on an old wooden bench under the open sky, Aurora let the tears she had been holding back flow freely. She looked up at the stars, whispering a prayer to Clara and Victor, asking them why they had left her and where they might be.

As if the heavens had heard her despair, it began to rain. The drops were soft at first, mingling with her tears, but soon turned into a heavy downpour. Aurora stayed where she was, letting the rain soak her completely. She felt too fragile to move, too lost to care about the chill creeping into her bones.

The night grew darker, and the park emptied as others fled for shelter. Aurora, drenched and trembling, sat alone. Her grief, compounded by the solitude, was suffocating her. The thought of returning to her cold, empty room was unbearable. She stayed in the park all night, crying softly until exhaustion overcame her.

By morning, Aurora's body was weak, and her throat burned. She had caught a fever from the cold rain. Stumbling back to her room, she rested briefly before visiting a nearby clinic known for its affordable rates. The clinic was small and crowded, with a weary-looking doctor managing a line of patients alongside three assistants. The doctor, Dr. Prakash, seemed helpful at first, but Aurora's sharp intuition soon caught something unsettling in his demeanor.

Each visit, his gaze lingered too long, and his questions grew unnecessarily personal. He began suggesting Aurora visit the clinic even when her symptoms were mild, offering free medicine and private consultations. She sensed his intentions were far from professional, and a chill ran down her spine each time she felt his predatory eyes on her.

The day he leaned too close while handing her a prescription, Aurora knew she couldn't go back. Her instincts screamed that he was waiting for the moment she'd be alone and vulnerable. She decided to stop visiting the clinic entirely, even if it meant enduring her recurring fevers without treatment.

As Aurora lay in her room that evening, her body shivering and her heart heavy with despair, she realized how vulnerable her situation had become. She was alone, young, and trying to survive in a world that seemed determined to break her spirit. Yet, even in her darkest moments, a small, persistent light flickered inside her—a determination to keep going, to fight for a life that honored the love and values Clara and Victor had instilled in her.

With that faint hope, Aurora resolved to find a way out of her struggles, no matter how impossible it seemed. She clutched the Tarot deck in her bag, wondering if the answers she desperately needed might lie within its mystical cards.

The following evening, as Aurora made her way back to her small rented room, the weight of her struggles hung heavily on her shoulders. She was exhausted—both physically and emotionally—when something caught her eye. Pinned to a street noticeboard was a simple paper advertisement:

"Vacancy at Horizon Bookstore. Female employee needed. Inquire within."

Her heart skipped a beat. It wasn't just a job opportunity—it was a glimmer of hope. Without hesitation, she noted the address and hurried to the bookstore. Desperation pushed her forward; she knew she had to seize this chance.

When she reached Horizon Bookstore, the cozy warmth of the shop immediately lifted her spirits. Shelves filled with books stretched to the ceiling, and the faint scent of old pages mingled with the aroma of freshly brewed coffee from a small counter nearby. It was unlike anything Aurora had ever seen before—a world of knowledge and stories, all waiting to be discovered.

The owner, a middle-aged man with kind eyes named Mr. Aman Mehra, greeted her and asked a few basic questions. Aurora answered honestly, sharing her love for learning and her eagerness to work hard. Though she was nervous, her sincerity shone through, and Mr. Mehra smiled.

"You seem like a bright and genuine young girl. Let's give this a try. Come by tomorrow morning, and we'll get started."

Aurora couldn't believe it. Her heart raced with gratitude. For the first time in what felt like an eternity, she felt a spark of hope. As she stepped out of the shop, the memories of Clara and Victor flooded back. She remembered their dreams for her—to study in the city, to rise above the simple life they had known. The sight of all those books reminded her of their words, their encouragement, and their love.

That night, Aurora returned to her room with a renewed sense of purpose. She ate a hearty meal for the first time in days, feeling her strength slowly returning. As she lay on her bed, the memories of Clara filled her mind. She recalled a quiet evening in the village when Clara had pointed to the stars and whispered, ***"Aurora, honey, do you know that the stars see us, listen to us, and respond to us? They're always watching, guiding us in ways we can't always understand."***

Aurora clung to those words as tears welled in her eyes. She missed Clara and Victor deeply, but the thought that the stars might still be watching over her brought her some comfort. With a heart full of gratitude, she whispered a silent thank-you to the heavens before drifting into sleep.

That night, she dreamt of Clara and Victor. In her dream, they were back in the old village house, sitting on the porch and counting stars. Clara was laughing, her voice warm and familiar, while Victor leaned back in his chair, his face serene. Aurora felt their love wrapping around her like a protective blanket.

When she woke up the next morning, the dream lingered in her mind like a blessing. The sunlight streaming through her window seemed brighter, as if it carried a promise of new beginnings. Aurora got ready and walked to the bookstore with a lightness in her step.

Her first day at Horizon Bookstore was nothing short of magical. The moment she stepped in, she felt a deep connection to the space. The rows of books seemed to whisper promises of stories, wisdom, and solace. Mr. Mehra showed her how to organize the shelves, assist customers, and manage the counter. Aurora quickly grasped everything; her sharp mind and eagerness to learn made her a natural.

As the day went on, Aurora found herself drawn to the books, flipping through their pages during quiet moments. She thought about Clara and Victor's wish for her to continue her education, and a new determination sparked within her. While formal schooling was out of reach for now, she decided she would teach herself. Every book in the store was an opportunity, and every visitor a chance to learn something new.

That evening, as she closed up the shop, Aurora looked up at the night sky. The stars twinkled above, just as Clara had said they would.

"Thank you," she whispered, her voice filled with emotion. "Thank you for watching over me."

As she walked back to her room, she felt a warmth in her chest—a feeling she hadn't experienced in a long time. She was still grieving, still lonely, but she was also hopeful. The journey ahead would be difficult, but she had taken her first step.

And for the first time in what felt like forever, Aurora smiled as she welcomed the night. Tomorrow, she knew, was a new day filled with possibilities.

Chapter Three: The Spark of Learning

Aurora had settled into her routine at Horizon Bookstore, and it became her sanctuary. The quiet hum of turning pages, the earthy scent of old and new books, and the occasional murmur of customers created an environment where Aurora found solace. She would meticulously arrange the shelves and assist visitors, but during quiet moments, she would immerse herself in the world of books. Each page she turned added a spark to her curiosity and a balm to her aching heart.

One rainy afternoon, while she was restocking a shelf, a man entered the store. He was in his late thirties, with a kind demeanor and sharp, intelligent eyes. He approached the counter, scanning the titles displayed behind her.

"Excuse me," he said politely, "I'm looking for a specific book on cultural anthropology. Do you happen to have *Stories of Civilization* by Dr. Miles Everett?"

Aurora smiled, her hands dusted with the scent of paper. "Let me check the inventory," she said, walking swiftly to a nearby shelf. After a moment of searching, she retrieved the book and handed it to him.

The man nodded in appreciation. "Thank you. I'm Jonathan," he said. "I'm a professor at the State University, and I visit this store often. I've noticed you have a deep interest in books. May I ask, what are you studying?"

Aurora hesitated. The question touched a tender nerve. "I'm not studying right now," she admitted, her voice soft but steady. "I'm from a small village. I've finished my higher secondary education, and I love reading and learning about almost everything—technology, mythology, music, and art. But I can't afford higher education at the moment. So, I work here and save what I can. One day, I hope to continue studying."

Jonathan listened intently, his brow furrowed in thought. "You shouldn't let finances stop you," he said after a pause. "Education is within reach if you seek the right opportunities. Apply to a university—you can get a loan for tuition. I have a library of books I'd be happy to share with you. If you're willing to put in the effort, the ladder to your dreams is already within your grasp and along with this start meditation for sometime."

Aurora was taken aback by his encouragement. She had always dreamed of climbing higher, but the idea of someone supporting her seemed almost surreal. Still, his words ignited something within her—a long-buried hope.

A month later, Aurora applied to the State University. With Jonathan's help, she navigated the process of securing an education loan and prepared for the leap. On her first day, stepping onto the university campus felt like entering another world. She was nervous yet determined, her dreams beginning to take form.

Among her classmates, Aurora met Joy, a charismatic and outgoing boy from a wealthy family. Joy was drawn to Aurora's quiet determination and genuine nature, and their friendship blossomed quickly. He introduced her to the world of material wealth: lavish parties, elegant homes, and social circles buzzing with affluence. Aurora, while grateful for his company, always felt out of place in this world. She admired Joy's lifestyle but couldn't help feeling an emptiness in it. Deep down, she wanted to create her own path rather than ride on someone else's privilege.

Among the bustling chatter and lively activities of her classmates, Aurora found herself drawn to Joy, a boy whose vibrant energy seemed to light up every room he entered. Joy came from a wealthy family, and his confidence and charm were as magnetic as they were overwhelming. While Aurora's world was rooted in quiet resilience and a yearning for deeper purpose, Joy's life was a whirlwind of extravagance and excitement.

Joy was captivated by Aurora's authenticity. Unlike the other girls in his social circle, Aurora wasn't impressed by his designer clothes or flashy car. Her quiet determination, genuine kindness, and the way her eyes lit up when talking about her dreams intrigued him. He admired how she worked tirelessly toward her goals, even when the odds were against her.

The two began spending more time together, and their friendship blossomed into something special. Joy introduced Aurora to his world—a life of grandeur that she had only seen in movies. He took her to lavish parties, where chandeliers sparkled like starlight and laughter echoed through opulent halls. He invited her to his family's estate, a sprawling mansion with immaculately manicured gardens and rooms filled with priceless art.

Aurora was grateful for Joy's companionship and the window he provided into a different world. But while she appreciated the beauty and luxury, she couldn't shake a lingering sense of discomfort. The glittering facade of Joy's lifestyle felt hollow to her. She noticed how conversations at these gatherings often revolved around appearances and wealth, lacking the depth and sincerity she craved.

One evening, as they stood on a terrace overlooking Joy's estate, he said, "You know, Aurora, you belong in this world. I can see you thriving here."

Aurora smiled softly, but her heart tugged in another direction. *Belonging?* she wondered. *Or just passing through?*

She admired Joy's ease in this world but couldn't help feeling that her path lay elsewhere. She wanted to build her own life, to create something meaningful that went beyond wealth and privilege.

Over time, Joy and Aurora's friendship deepened. They spent hours talking about their dreams and fears. Joy often marveled at Aurora's strength and independence, while Aurora found solace in Joy's unwavering support.

One evening, after walking her home from a small café they frequented, Joy stopped at the gate and turned to her. "Aurora, there's something I've been wanting to say."

His voice was softer than usual, his usual confidence tinged with vulnerability. Aurora's heart quickened as he continued.

"I've fallen for you," he said, searching her eyes for a reaction. "You're unlike anyone I've ever met. You're grounded, honest, and full of dreams that inspire me. I love you."

Aurora froze for a moment, a mix of surprise and uncertainty washing over her. Love was something she had kept at arm's length, afraid it might distract her from her goals or lead to heartbreak.

"I don't know, Joy," she admitted hesitantly. "Our worlds are so different."

"I don't care about that," he replied, taking her hands in his. "I just care about you. Let's create our own world, together."

His sincerity melted her doubts, and for the first time, Aurora allowed herself to lean into the possibility of love.

Their relationship blossomed, filling Aurora's life with a new kind of joy and excitement. Joy became her safe haven, a place where she could laugh freely and feel supported. He introduced her to his favourite spots around the city, from hidden bookstores to scenic overlooks, and she shared with him her passion for meditation and spirituality.

On quiet evenings, they would sit on the beach, watching the waves roll in under the moonlight. Joy often spoke of their future, painting vivid pictures of a life where they could support each other and thrive together.

"I'll always stand by you," he promised one night, his arm around her. "No matter what."

For the first time in years, Aurora felt a connection that made her heart soar. Joy's presence gave her hope that love could coexist with her ambitions.

But as the months passed, cracks began to form in their seemingly perfect relationship. Joy's messages became less frequent, his once-endless enthusiasm dimming. Aurora tried to brush off her concerns, convincing herself that he was just busy.

Then, one night, everything unraveled. Aurora received a text message that shattered her world:

"I'm sorry, Aurora. I can't continue this relationship. I've met someone my family approves of, and she's from our circle. I hope you understand."

Aurora stared at the screen, her heart sinking. The words felt like a dagger, reopening old wounds she thought were beginning to heal. Joy had chosen a wealthy girl, one who fit neatly into his world, leaving Aurora behind without warning.

Her room felt suffocating that night as she lay in bed, tears streaming silently down her face. She questioned everything—her worth, her choices, and the stars that seemed to mock her pain.

Despite the heartbreak, Aurora resolved not to let this betrayal define her. She turned to meditation and her spiritual practices for solace, slowly piecing herself back together. Joy had taught her a valuable lesson about love and resilience, one that would shape her journey moving forward.

The pain, though overwhelming, became a catalyst for growth. Aurora began to focus more intently on her dreams, channeling her emotions into her spiritual practices and her ambitions. She vowed that when love came into her life again, it would be on her terms—rooted in mutual respect, understanding, and shared values.

This chapter of Aurora's life, though bittersweet, would serve as a reminder of her strength and her unwavering commitment to forging her own path.

But Aurora was no stranger to resilience. Betrayal and loneliness had taught her how to survive. Wiping her tears, she made a vow to herself:

I will never depend on anyone for my happiness or success again. The stars may want me to walk this journey alone, and if that's the case, I'll embrace it. I will build my life on my own terms.

From that day forward, Aurora poured all her energy into her studies. She spent hours in the library, absorbing knowledge and excelling in her coursework. She avoided relationships and focused solely on her goals, determined to prove her strength to herself.

Aurora was no longer the girl waiting for someone to save her. She was becoming a woman who would forge her destiny, even if it meant walking the path alone.

Aurora sat in the cozy corner of her favorite café, a notebook open in front of her and a warm cappuccino by her side. The café was alive with its usual chatter and the soft hum of music, but Aurora was lost in her thoughts, jotting down ideas for her future. She barely noticed the fading sunlight outside until the room suddenly plunged into darkness.

All the lights went out at once. Startled murmurs filled the café, but Aurora's heart clenched with a sudden chill. The darkness felt unnatural, heavy, and suffocating. Her breathing quickened as an icy voice echoed in the void around her.

"Aurora," the voice called, deep and menacing. It was Zalarak.

She froze in her seat, her heart pounding as she realized she couldn't see anything—not even her own hands. The world around her had dissolved into pitch-black nothingness. She tried to focus, summoning every ounce of courage she had.

"Did you really think you were safe?" Zalarak's voice sneered, coming closer. "Even here, in this little corner of the mortal world, I can reach you. No light can protect you from me."

Aurora gripped the edge of the table, her mind racing. She opened her mouth to speak, but her words caught in her throat. She felt his oppressive energy closing in, suffocating her resolve.

"Your protector is absent, Aurora," Zalarak continued. "You're alone now. Weak. Vulnerable. And I'll destroy you."

Suddenly, a loud clattering sound broke the spell of his words. The café staff had managed to restore the power. Light flooded the room, blinding Aurora momentarily. She blinked rapidly, her heart still racing, but when her vision cleared, Zalarak was gone.

Her eyes darted around the café, but no trace of him remained. The patrons were murmuring about the blackout, oblivious to the sinister encounter that had just transpired. Aurora sat motionless, her hands trembling. Was she losing her mind, or had it really happened?

Before she could collect herself, a man approached her table. He was tall and enigmatic, with a calm yet powerful presence that instantly caught her attention. His eyes were kind but held a deep intensity.

"Aurora," he said softly, his voice steady and grounding.

She stared at him, her pulse still erratic. "Who—who are you?" she stammered.

"I'm sent by Jonathan," he said, placing a small object on the table in front of her. It was a crystal ball, glowing faintly with an ethereal light. "He said to give this to you and to tell you—never part with it. Keep it close at all times. It will shield you."

Aurora's gaze shifted between the crystal ball and the stranger. "Jonathan sent you?" she asked, her voice trembling. "But who are you? Why now?"

He smiled faintly. "My name is Evander. Jonathan knew this moment would come, and he prepared for it. You're no longer safe without this." His tone was grave, yet reassuring.

Aurora took the crystal ball into her hands, its cool surface pulsing faintly as if alive. "What does it do?" she whispered.

Evander stood back, his expression unreadable. "You'll find out when you need to. For now, trust me—and trust Jonathan. The battle is far from over."

With those words, Evander turned and disappeared into the bustling café crowd. Aurora clutched the crystal ball, her mind spinning with fear, confusion, and questions. The encounter with Zalarak, Evander's sudden appearance, and Jonathan's cryptic message—it was all too much.

But one thing was clear: she was no longer an ordinary girl sipping coffee in a café. The darkness was closing in, and the fight for her survival—and perhaps much more—was just beginning.

Chapter Four: The Mystical Encounter

The same night, In Aurora's dream, Aurora walked briskly down the dimly lit street. Rain poured in relentless sheets, soaking her coat and dripping from the edges of her umbrella. The air was heavy with an unshakable sense of unease, a feeling that had plagued her since her strange encounter with the man in the coffee shop. It wasn't just his words that unsettled her but the persistent sensation that someone—or something—was shadowing her every move.

The feeling clung to her like a second skin as if a shadow loomed just beyond her vision. She glanced over her shoulder, but the street was empty save for the occasional passerby, their umbrellas bobbing against the rain.

Turning the corner, she stopped abruptly. Her eyes fell upon a small, weathered sign hanging above a door that looked out of place in the modern city surroundings.

"Ethereal Tomes: Books & Mysteries"

The shop seemed to glow faintly, its fogged windows flickering with candlelight. Drawn by something she couldn't explain, Aurora pushed open the creaky door, a bell tinkling softly above her.

Inside, the air was warm and heavy with the scent of old parchment and burning incense. Shelves crammed with books of all sizes stretched to the ceiling, their spines embossed with strange symbols and unfamiliar languages. Tapestries hung on the walls, their patterns weaving stories of mythical battles and celestial alignments.

"Welcome," a melodic voice called out from behind the counter.

Aurora turned to see a woman emerging from the shadows. She was striking, with fiery red hair cascading over her shoulders and piercing green eyes that seemed to see straight through Aurora's guarded demeanor.

"I'm Tessa," the woman said, a knowing smile on her lips. "And you've been expected."

Aurora frowned, her unease growing. "Expected? I don't understand. I just... stumbled in here."

Tessa tilted her head, her smile widening. "Stumbled, or were guided?" She gestured to a cozy corner of the shop, where a table draped in deep velvet stood. On it lay an ornate Tarot deck, its edges gilded in gold. Candles flickered around it, casting eerie shadows.

"Sit," Tessa said softly.

Despite her reservations, Aurora found herself moving toward the table, her body responding to a pull she couldn't resist.

"I see the portal is open," Tessa began as she shuffled the cards with practiced ease. "And they've started to find you."

"Portal? Who's finding me?" Aurora asked, her voice trembling.

"You're not just anyone, Aurora. The other realm has waited a long time for you to take your rightful place. But with that comes responsibility—and danger."

Aurora's heart raced. "I don't understand what you're saying. Who are you? How do you know my name?"

Tessa didn't answer directly. Instead, she laid three cards in a spread before Aurora. The images on them were vivid and otherworldly, unlike any Tarot deck Aurora had ever seen.

"The first card," Tessa said, turning it over, "represents your past." It was **The Star**, shimmering in hues of gold and blue. "You've always been guided by hope, even when surrounded by darkness. Mother Nature herself has sheltered you, and the shining thread you carry has been your shield."

Aurora stared at the card, her breath hitching.

"The second card is your present," Tessa continued, flipping the next card. **The Tower**. Lightning split the sky on the card, a structure crumbling under its fury. "Chaos surrounds you, doesn't it? The upheaval is necessary for your awakening."

Aurora's chest tightened. Everything in her life had indeed fallen apart—first Clara and Victor, then the betrayal by Joy, and now the eerie encounters and inexplicable feelings.

"And the final card," Tessa said, revealing **The High Priestess**. A woman sat serenely, flanked by pillars of light and dark. "This is your future, Aurora. You are destined to hold immense wisdom and power, but only if you embrace who you truly are."

Aurora shook her head, her voice barely audible. "I don't understand any of this."

Tessa reached across the table, taking Aurora's trembling hands in hers. "The shining thread and locket you wearing—the one gifted to you—it has served its purpose.

It kept you hidden and protected for 21 years. But now, you must bury it in the earth. Its job is done, and the time has come for you to stand on your own. Use the Tarot deck you've carried all these years, there is a booklet in the box of deck, start using it. It's not just a tool; it's your guide, your connection to what lies ahead."

"Protected me?" Aurora whispered, her mind reeling. *"From what?"*

Tessa's eyes softened. *"From forces you can't yet comprehend. But I promise, when the time is right, you'll understand everything. Prepare yourself, Aurora. The battles ahead are great, but so is your strength."*

Before Aurora could respond, a strange dizziness overcame her. The shop blurred, and when she blinked, she found herself alone in her room, clutching the Tarot deck that had always been with her.

Confused and shaken, she opened the deck for the first time in years. As if compelled, she shuffled the cards and drew one for guidance.

Her hand trembled as she revealed the card: **The Sun.**

Aurora's breath caught. The radiant image on the card seemed to glow brighter than she remembered, its golden hues shining with an almost ethereal brilliance. A child rode a white horse under a blazing sun, arms spread wide in joyous abandon. Behind them, a wall of sunflowers stood tall, their faces turned toward the light.

The card exuded warmth, hope, and clarity. It was a symbol of illumination, success, and the triumph of truth over darkness. Aurora felt an overwhelming surge of energy, as though the sun depicted on the card was shining directly on her, chasing away the shadows that had clouded her heart.

For the first time in what felt like an eternity, Aurora felt a flicker of warmth and hope.

She studied the card, its imagery speaking to her on a level that words couldn't. The Sun was a promise of brighter days ahead, a reminder that no matter how dark the night, the dawn would always come. The child on the horse represented purity and optimism, untainted by fear or doubt. The white horse symbolized the strength of her inner spirit, carrying her forward with unwavering resolve.

In that moment, Aurora realized that the universe was still guiding her. Even when she felt lost and broken, the stars—and now the cards—were watching over her, offering reassurance that she wasn't entirely in the dark.

The Sun card was not just a beacon of hope but also a call to action. It urged her to embrace her own light, to trust in her strength and abilities. Whatever challenges lay ahead, she had the power to overcome them, to rise above the chaos and reclaim her path.

Aurora clutched the card to her chest, tears streaming down her face. They weren't tears of sorrow, but of release—a letting go of the fear and doubt that had weighed her down. The Sun reminded her that she was not alone, that her journey was far from over, and that her destiny was still hers to shape.

Aurora awoke the morning after her vivid dream of Tessa with a lingering sense of purpose and restlessness. The world around her seemed alive in ways she couldn't explain. The rustle of leaves outside her window sounded like murmured secrets, and the sunlight streaming through the curtains felt warmer, almost reassuring.

But the changes within her were even more profound. Her heightened intuition had deepened to a startling degree. She could sense emotions and energies around her with startling clarity—a colleague's irritation, the quiet sorrow of a stranger, or the innocent joy of a child playing across the street. These feelings resonated deeply, leaving her overwhelmed yet intrigued.

Despite her unease, Aurora's pragmatic nature urged her to maintain her focus. She decided to visit the university, eager to meet Sir Jonathan. The questions swirling in her mind wouldn't let her rest: Who was the stranger in the café, the man who appeared in the darkness? Why had Jonathan sent her the crystal ball? And what role did Tessa play in all of this?

When Aurora arrived at the university, however, she learned that Professor Jonathan was on leave. Disappointed but undeterred, she resolved to make the most of her day. She spent hours in the library, poring over books on metaphysics, energy systems, and ancient myths, hoping to find clues that could illuminate her path.

Yet, even as she immersed herself in her studies, the questions wouldn't relent. Who was the stranger, and what did he want from her? What was the true purpose of the crystal ball Jonathan had sent? And why was Tessa, the enigmatic figure in her dreams, so central to the mysteries unfolding around her?

As she walked home that evening, her mind swirled with possibilities. She realized that finding Jonathan wasn't just about getting answers—it was about uncovering the truth of her growing connection to a world she was only beginning to understand.

Every night, Aurora gazed at the crystal ball resting on her bedside table, its soft, ethereal light spreading across her room like a protective embrace. The gentle glow painted the walls in hues of serenity, casting away every shadow. As she drifted to sleep in its soothing radiance, Aurora felt a profound sense of safety, as if the crystal was shielding her from the darkness that once loomed in her life. In its light, she found peace, a constant reminder that she was never truly alone.

Aurora's dedication bore fruit when her final results were announced. She had graduated at the top of her class and received an offer for a prestigious management position in a reputed company. The salary was generous, allowing her to live comfortably while also pursuing her passion projects.

Her work at the company demanded her full attention, especially in board meetings dominated by older, influential men who were quick to dismiss her ideas. Despite the odds, Aurora held her ground. Her presentations were insightful, her strategies innovative, and her execution flawless. Each victory in the corporate jungle was hard-won, yet bittersweet.

In the evenings, Aurora continued her association with the state university, teaching a monthly lecture on the applications of modern technology. It became her escape— a space where young, curious minds reminded her of her own struggles and dreams. The small honorarium she earned from these sessions was donated entirely to a fund she had created for underprivileged children who couldn't afford an education.

This act of giving filled Aurora with purpose. She often remembered Clara and Victor's wish for her to create a life of meaning and impact. Her rapport with the university staff and students grew steadily, and many admired her for her wisdom, kindness, and humility.

However, her time in the corporate world left her disillusioned. In boardrooms filled with posturing and ego, Aurora noticed how shallow judgments based on gender, appearance, and social status overshadowed meaningful ideas and innovation. Her brilliance was respected but grudgingly acknowledged.

Aurora began to see how people were trapped in a superficial world, clinging to hierarchies and facades while neglecting their inner light. She longed for an environment where people were valued for their authenticity, creativity, and passion—not their titles or bank balances.

One night, after another grueling day at work, Aurora sat with a notebook, scribbling her thoughts and frustrations. She envisioned a space where ideas flowed freely, where people could grow and thrive without fear of judgment. Slowly, the idea began to crystallize: she would start her own company, one that would champion innovation, mindfulness, and purpose.

Aurora shared her idea with a few close colleagues whom she trusted deeply. These were people who had become her friends, allies in a corporate world that often felt cold and impersonal. They had seen her navigate challenges with grace and admired her for her relentless passion and grounded nature.

"You have everything it takes to make this happen," said Mia, one of her closest confidantes. "Your vision, your work ethic, and your ability to inspire people—it's all there."

"Do it," added Raj, another colleague. "I've been thinking about leaving this place anyway. If you start something new, I'll be the first to join you."

Their encouragement lit a spark within Aurora. She began creating a mind map of her business idea, outlining the core values, services, and goals. She envisioned a tech and innovation firm that would integrate mindfulness and ethical practices into its operations.

"I don't just want to make profits," Aurora explained to her friends one evening over coffee. "I want to build something meaningful. A company where people can collaborate with purpose, where they feel seen and valued—not judged by their appearance or background."

Aurora's plan began to take shape over the next few weeks. She worked late into the night, balancing her current job while laying the foundation for her dream. Her connections at the university proved invaluable, as professors and students offered insights into emerging technologies and trends.

Though the road ahead was daunting, Aurora felt a newfound clarity. The stars, it seemed, were aligning for her once again. And deep in her heart, she knew this was only the beginning of a journey that would transform not just her life, but the lives of many others.

The memory of Clara's voice echoed in her mind: *"The stars see us, listen to us, understand us, and respond to us."*

Aurora gazed out of her window that night, the city lights twinkling like the stars she had once counted with Clara and Victor. She whispered a quiet prayer of gratitude, knowing they would always guide her, even in their absence.

Tomorrow, she would take her first steps toward building her dream.

Chapter Five: Awakening the Inner Flame

That night, as Aurora sat in her room, her heart was filled with both anticipation and doubt about the path she was about to embark on. The idea of starting her own company, of creating a space that resonated with her values, was both thrilling and terrifying. She felt a deep need for clarity, a sign that she was on the right path.

Sitting by the soft glow of a single lamp, Aurora reached for the tarot deck that had been her silent companion since she left the village. It had always been a source of comfort and wisdom, its cards holding mysteries that seemed to connect her to something greater than herself.

She shuffled the deck slowly, her fingers moving instinctively. Closing her eyes, she whispered to the stars, *"Guide me, as you always have. Show me what I need to know for this journey ahead."*

Laying the cards down, Aurora drew three cards for her spread: **The Fool**, **The Star**, and **The Queen of Pentacles**.

The first card, ***The Fool***, gleamed with its vibrant depiction of a young traveler standing at the edge of a cliff, ready to step into the unknown.

Aurora stared at the card, its meaning clear. It spoke of new beginnings, of taking a leap of faith. The Fool wasn't about recklessness—it was about trusting the journey, even when the path seemed uncertain.

"You are about to start something entirely new," Aurora thought, as if the card itself was speaking to her. *"It's time

to embrace the adventure with courage, knowing that the universe is guiding you."

This card felt like an affirmation of the leap she was about to take by starting her own company.

The second card, **The Star**, shone like a beacon of hope. A serene figure poured water from two vessels, connecting the earth and the heavens under a sky full of stars.

Aurora felt her heart lighten as she looked at the card. It represented inspiration, hope, and divine guidance. It reminded her of the nights she had spent with Clara and Victor, counting stars and whispering her dreams to them.

"You are not alone," the card seemed to say. *"Your path is blessed, and your vision will guide not just yourself, but others as well. Trust in your dreams, for they are aligned with something greater."*

Aurora smiled softly, a tear slipping down her cheek. The Star was a reminder that even in her moments of doubt, the universe was listening, guiding her steps.

The final card, **The Queen of Pentacles**, depicted a regal woman holding a golden coin, surrounded by lush greenery.

Aurora immediately understood its message. The Queen symbolized balance, nurturing, and the ability to create a life of abundance through hard work and care. It wasn't just about material success—it was about building something meaningful and sustainable.

"You have the ability to create prosperity, not just for yourself, but for those around you," Aurora thought. "You can combine wisdom with compassion, building a foundation that serves a greater purpose."

This card felt like a reflection of her deepest desires—to create a space where people could thrive, a company built on principles of mindfulness, innovation, and generosity.

Aurora sat back, gazing at the three cards spread before her. Together, they painted a clear picture:

The Fool urged her to take the leap and trust the journey ahead. **The Star** reminded her that she was guided and supported by forces greater than herself. **The Queen of Pentacles** assured her that she had the strength to create a life of abundance and purpose.

The cards felt like a roadmap, giving her the courage to move forward. She carefully placed them back into the deck, whispering a quiet thank-you to the stars and whatever force had guided her.

The next morning, Aurora woke up with a sense of clarity. The doubts that had clouded her mind were now replaced with determination. She gathered her notes and began refining her plan, preparing to take the first steps toward her dream.

Though the road ahead was uncertain, Aurora knew she was ready. The cards had spoken, and the stars above seemed to twinkle in agreement. A new chapter was about to unfold, and she was ready to write it with all the courage and passion within her.

Aurora's days were filled with relentless focus as she worked on her dream of starting her own company. Her evenings were spent planning strategies, coordinating with her colleagues, and refining her vision. The support from her trusted friends encouraged her, and their shared excitement made the journey feel less daunting.

But amidst the hustle of the physical world, Aurora's mind often wandered back to the mystical encounters she had experienced. She couldn't shake the memory of Tessa and her cryptic guidance. Who was Tessa, really? What did she mean by *realms* and Aurora's role in bridging them? The questions gnawed at her, especially in the stillness of the night.

One such night, after an exhausting day of work and planning, Aurora found herself lying awake. Her thoughts swirled like a storm: the excitement of her company, the mystery of Tessa, and the strange power she was beginning to sense within herself. As sleep overtook her, the veil between the worlds thinned.

In her dream, she found herself in a luminous garden under a canopy of stars. The air was thick with the scent of blooming flowers, and the atmosphere pulsed with a serene energy. There, standing amidst the glowing flora, was Tessa.

"You called me," Tessa said softly, her voice a blend of warmth and authority.

Aurora nodded, her words tumbling out in a rush. *"I don't understand what's happening. Why do I feel so connected to something I can't explain? Who am I, really? And why do you keep saying I have a role in balancing realms?"*

Tessa's gaze was steady, her presence calming. *"You are doing well, Aurora. Your journey in the material world is important—it will ground you, teach you, and strengthen you. But you must also delve deeper into the spiritual truth of your existence. You are not just here for the earthly realm; you are here to bridge the balance between realms."*

Aurora's heart pounded. *"How do I search for this truth? I don't even know where to begin."*

Tessa smiled gently. *"You begin by listening—to your intuition, to the signs around you, and to the whispers of your soul. The answers will come when you seek with genuine intent. You must trust yourself and the universe."*

Before Aurora could ask more, the dream began to fade, and Tessa's parting words lingered: *"I will always come when you need me. Call me with your heart, and I will answer."*

Aurora woke with a start. Her heart raced as she replayed the dream in her mind. Though her questions weren't fully answered, something had shifted within her. There was a sense of clarity—not of the mind, but of the soul.

She sat up in her bed and closed her eyes, trying to recapture the energy of the dream. Suddenly, she became acutely aware of her own presence—not just her physical body, but something deeper. It was as if she could see her soul, radiant and distinct from her human form.

The experience was both humbling and empowering. She felt a divine connection within herself, a quiet but unshakable strength that she had never noticed before. Though she couldn't fully articulate it, she understood the essence of it by heart.

"I am more than I've ever realized," Aurora whispered to herself. *"And yet, there's so much more to uncover."*

The morning sun streamed through her window, and Aurora felt different. She was still the same person—determined to build her company and create a meaningful life—but there was a new layer of purpose behind her actions.

She went about her day with a renewed sense of power. In meetings, she spoke with confidence, her words resonating with an unseen energy. When working on her company plans, she felt ideas flow effortlessly, as if guided by an invisible hand.

And yet, the questions remained, lingering at the edge of her mind like a tantalizing mystery. Who was she, truly? What did Tessa mean by *realms* and *balance*?

Aurora knew she couldn't force the answers to come. Instead, she decided to focus on the journey itself, trusting that each step would bring her closer to understanding.

By the end of the week, Aurora's colleagues noticed something different about her. There was a glow in her demeanor, a quiet confidence that seemed to draw people toward her. She was a natural leader, not just because of her skills, but because of the energy she exuded.

But Aurora kept her inner experiences to herself. She wasn't ready to share the depth of what she was feeling— not yet. For now, she was content to let her actions speak louder than her words.

As she stood by her window that evening, gazing at the stars, she whispered, *"I don't know where this path will lead, but I'm ready. I trust you, stars. I trust the journey."*

And for the first time in a long while, Aurora felt at peace. The power within her was growing, and she was beginning to understand that the universe had plans far greater than anything she could imagine.

Aurora's life was a whirlwind of ambition, mystery, and growing inner power, but amidst the chaos, shadows began to follow her—both literal and metaphorical.

It was a rainy evening as Aurora walked back to her apartment from work. The streets were dimly lit, the occasional puddle reflecting the soft glow of streetlights. She felt a prickle of awareness, like eyes boring into her. Looking across the road, she caught sight of a figure. They weren't approaching her, but their presence was unmistakable.

Aurora's heart raced, but not with fear. Instead, a deep sense of curiosity and caution gripped her. The figure didn't attempt to cross or call out; they simply followed at a distance. She quickened her pace, determined to get home, but in her mind, she filed away the encounter.

The next evening, Aurora stopped by the coffee shop she frequented to escape the rain. As she sipped her drink and reviewed her plans for the company, her thoughts wandered back to the figure from the night before. Just then, the coffee shop door jingled, and the same person walked in who was watching Aurora last evening.

Aurora's heart skipped a beat. The man scanned the room and, upon spotting her, made his way over. He sat across from her without asking for permission, his face partially hidden by a hood.

"It's me, Aurora," he said, his voice low.

Aurora tilted her head, trying to place him. "I'm sorry, but... do I know you?"

Before she could get an answer, he glanced nervously toward the door. "They're watching. If they find me again, they'll kill me."

"Who?" Aurora asked, leaning forward, but the man abruptly stood.

"I just wanted to share something, but it's not safe. I'll come back when I can," he muttered before disappearing into the rain-soaked night.

Aurora sat there, stunned. Her mind was awash with questions. Who was he? What did he mean by *they*? Why did it feel like she was at the center of something larger than herself, yet completely in the dark?

Despite the strange encounters, Aurora's focus returned to her company. The ambitious project required every ounce of her energy, and she poured herself into her work. But the mysteries that surrounded her refused to fade.

Aurora had learned to rely on her inner strength. She spoke to the stars in her heart, leaving her unanswered questions to their wisdom. *What I don't understand, I give it to you to handle,* she often whispered in her quiet moments.

The mounting responsibilities took a toll on Aurora. Her job demanded excellence, and her dream of starting a company required relentless effort. She had become known for her meticulous work and dedication, but one day, in the chaos of her dual commitments, a critical deadline slipped past her unnoticed.

Her boss called her into his office. His voice was sharp, his words cutting.

"Aurora, this isn't like you. You've been missing details, losing focus. If this continues, let me know if you even want to work here anymore."

Aurora sat silently, the sting of his words piercing her heart. She had given everything to the company—her time, her energy, even her health at times. And yet, a single mistake had erased all her past contributions in his eyes.

She returned to her desk, the weight of the reprimand heavy on her shoulders. As much as it hurt, she realized the truth in his words. She had taken on more than she could handle, constantly pushing herself to meet impossible standards without a break.

"I've been trying to do it all," Aurora thought, "but at what cost? Respect should not come at the expense of my well-being or dignity."

That evening, Aurora sat by her window, gazing at the stars. She replayed the events of the day, feeling the bruises of her boss's words and her own relentless self-expectations.

"I am not perfect," she whispered to the night sky. "But I am capable. And I deserve to be valued—not just for what I do, but for who I am."

The stars seemed to wink in response, as if assuring her that she was heard.

From that moment, Aurora resolved to recalibrate her priorities. She would honour her responsibilities but not at the expense of her self-worth. She would channel her energy into her company, where she could create something of her own—a place where respect and value were intrinsic, not conditional.

As she turned off the lights and climbed into bed, a new determination settled within her. Aurora knew the path ahead would be challenging, but she also knew that she carried within her the power to forge her destiny. And for now, that was enough.

Empowered by the transformative guidance of The **Sun card**, Aurora made a bold decision to reshape her life. She resigned from her current job, thanking the journey that had brought her this far but realizing it no longer aligned with her true calling. With a newfound sense of purpose, she launched her own company, one rooted in her vision of blending material success with spiritual growth. Her business would not only aim to thrive financially but also inspire individuals to discover their inner strength and light. With renewed zeal and energy, Aurora stepped into this new chapter, determined to build something extraordinary that reflected her soul's purpose.

Chapter Six: The Cards of Guidance

Aurora sat by her window, the city lights twinkling like scattered stars. The air was heavy with her emotions—hope, uncertainty, and a touch of anxiety. Her journey toward independence had begun, but she knew the path was fraught with challenges. Tonight, as she often did in moments of doubt, she turned to her Tarot deck for clarity.

The deck felt warm in her hands as she shuffled, her thoughts swirling with questions. She had already invested everything she had—her savings, her energy, and her trust in her team of ten. The campaigns for her tech products had generated some buzz, but the real breakthrough would come only with support from major investors. And now, with competitors attempting to tarnish her company's image, she felt the weight of the battle ahead.

Aurora closed her eyes, took a deep breath, and whispered her intention: What lies ahead for my company, and how can I overcome the obstacles in my way? She drew three cards.

Aurora's heart skipped a beat as she flipped the first card. **The Magician** stood before her, radiating confidence and mastery. The card spoke of her potential, her ability to manifest her vision into reality.

"You have all the tools you need," she murmured, interpreting the card. The message was clear: she had the knowledge, skills, and resources to shape her destiny. But she would need to channel her focus and believe in her power to turn ideas into action.

The next card **Five of Wands** depicted a chaotic scene of conflict—a group of people locked in a struggle. Aurora frowned. She knew this card symbolized competition and challenges.

"This is what I'm facing," she thought. Her competitors were not only rivals in the market but also forces actively trying to undermine her. The card reminded her that while conflict was inevitable, it could also be an opportunity to grow stronger, to prove her worth, and to refine her strategies.

A sense of peace washed over her as she revealed the final card. **The Star**, with its serene and hopeful energy, filled her with renewed strength.

"The light at the end of the tunnel," she whispered. The Star was a beacon of guidance, a reminder that despite the darkness, hope and inspiration were always within reach. It encouraged her to stay true to her vision and to trust in her journey, even when the path seemed unclear.

Aurora placed the cards back in the deck, her mind clearer than it had been in days. The Magician told her to trust her abilities, the Five of Wands reminded her to rise above the competition, and the Star urged her to keep faith in her dreams.

With this renewed determination, Aurora doubled down on her efforts. She and her team re-evaluated their strategies, focusing on innovation and authenticity. They launched a new campaign highlighting the unique aspects of their products, leveraging the trust they had built with their existing customers.

Aurora also reached out to potential investors with a refined pitch, showcasing the resilience and potential of her company. Her passion and sincerity left an impression, and she managed to secure meetings with a few major investors.

As her company grew, so did the challenges. False rumors and negative reviews from competitors began to circulate. Aurora knew these tactics were designed to shake her resolve, but she refused to give in.

She addressed the defamation head-on, using transparency and open communication to build trust with her customers. Her team worked tirelessly to maintain the quality and reliability of their products, ensuring that their actions spoke louder than the words of their detractors.

Aurora's journey was not without setbacks, but she had learned to view obstacles as stepping stones. The lessons from her Tarot cards echoed in her heart, reminding her of her strength, her resourcefulness, and the guiding light that always shone within her.

With every challenge she overcame, Aurora grew not just as a businesswoman but as a person. She was creating more than a company—she was building a legacy, one guided by wisdom, perseverance, and the stars that had always watched over her.

Aurora's mind was heavy with unanswered questions as she walked home from another long day at the office. The persistent silence from potential investors gnawed at her, adding to her frustration. The competitive market had not been kind, and her dreams of growing her company felt like they were slipping further away.

The evening was unusually still, with the rain clouds from earlier having given way to a cold, dark sky. As she turned a corner, she saw him again—the stranger who had spoken cryptically to her twice before. His presence sent a ripple of unease through her.

This time, there was no hesitation. He crossed the street quickly, grabbing her by the arm and pulling her into the shadows of a nearby shop. The dim light inside cast eerie patterns on the walls, and the air was thick with tension.

The man's voice was urgent, trembling but firm. "Listen to me carefully, Aurora. You're running out of time."

Aurora looked at him with narrowed eyes, her frustration boiling over. "Who are you? And why are you following me?"

"I am Elias," he replied, his voice hushed. "I've been trying to reach you because you're in danger. Dark forces are closing in on you—they want to strip you of your power, your light, and your destiny."

Aurora froze, her breath catching at the sound of the name. "Elias?" she whispered, her voice barely audible. Her eyes widened in disbelief as she took a step closer, her mind racing. "It can't be... Elias? Where have you been? What happened to you? I thought you were gone forever!"

Aurora's brows furrowed, her skepticism clear. "What forces? What power? You're talking in riddles. If there's a threat, let them come. I'll face them."

Elias shook his head, his face pale with fear. "You don't understand. These forces are not of this world. They've captured everyone who's tried to help you. They want you isolated, weak, and doubting yourself. They know you're growing stronger, and that terrifies them. You are destined to rule over **Etheria**, Aurora. But they want to destroy you before you can claim your throne."

Aurora blinked, the name **Etheria** ringing like a faint echo in her mind. She had not heard it before—Tessa had not mentioned it in her dreams.

"Tessa… what do you know about her?" Aurora demanded, her tone sharpening.

"She's waiting for you," Elias said quickly. "She's been protecting you, guiding you. She's your—"

Suddenly, Elias was yanked backward, his words cut off mid-sentence. A gust of cold, dark air filled the shop, and Aurora stumbled back, shielding her eyes. When she opened them, Elias was gone.

The silence that followed was deafening, broken only by a deep, malevolent voice that seemed to seep from the shadows themselves.

"I will come for you, Aurora. You cannot escape me. I am the only King. And only I rule."

Aurora stood frozen, her heart pounding in her chest. The voice was chilling, laced with a darkness that felt ancient and overwhelming.

As the eerie presence faded, Aurora steadied herself, her fear morphing into determination. She clenched her fists, her voice firm as she spoke aloud to the empty shop.

"If you want me, come and face me. I will not run. I will not hide."

She left the shop with her mind racing, replaying the cryptic warnings Elias had given her. Who was he? Why was he taken? And who—or what—was the dark force threatening her?

As she stepped back into the night, the faintest glimmer of light caught her eye—a single star twinkling in the otherwise cloudy sky.

Tessa is helping me, Aurora thought, her heart finding a fragile thread of comfort. And she's waiting for me in Etheria.

Aurora knew she needed answers, and she resolved to uncover the truth. But for now, her focus was clear: she would protect what she had built, she would face any challenge that came her way, and she would not let fear dictate her destiny.

What she didn't realize was that this was just the beginning of a much larger battle—one that would challenge not only her strength but the very essence of who she was meant to be.

Aurora lay in her bed, her thoughts drifting between Tessa and Elias. As sleep embraced her, Tessa appeared once more in her dream, unraveling deeper secrets. The name Zalarak resonated like a distant thunder in her mind, and the gravity of Tessa's revelations settled heavily on her heart. For years, Aurora had journeyed through life believing her battles were hers alone. Now, she was beginning to see the threads of her struggles woven into a much larger tapestry—a destiny far greater than she had ever imagined.

Tessa's voice was still fresh in her mind:

"Zalarak, the malevolent ruler of the Realm of Darkness, thrives where light cannot reach. A master of all dark energies, he draws his immense power from shadows, despair, and fear, growing stronger in complete darkness. His aura is oppressive, chilling, and suffocating, as though the very air bends to his will. Zalarak's hatred for light stems from his deep-rooted fear and envy of its purity, strength, and the hope it brings to others—a power he cannot control or corrupt.

As the sworn enemy of Etheria, Zalarak's existence is a perpetual threat to its harmony and balance. He is driven by a corrosive mix of negative ego and paranoia, a dangerous combination that fuels his relentless pursuit to snuff out light wherever it emerges. He envisions a world consumed by darkness, where fear and chaos reign, and he sits unchallenged as its ruler.

Zalarak's betrayal runs deep. It was his deceit and cruelty that led to the death of Aurora's parents, who had stood as protectors of light and Etheria's peace. Their demise was not only a personal loss for Aurora but also a calculated move by Zalarak to eliminate all who opposed his rise. His power, cunning, and ruthlessness make him a formidable enemy, one whose very presence shakes the core of Etheria."

Zalarak's grip on the realms of light was suffocating, a sinister force that loomed over Etheria like a storm cloud. He had infiltrated every corner, spreading his darkness to extinguish even the faintest flicker of hope. The once-thriving realms of light, known for their beauty and harmony, now lay in shadows, their guardians defeated or imprisoned under his reign. Yet, whispers of rebellion persisted. Brave souls, devoted to the light, worked in secrecy, smuggling messages and resources to Aurora.

They knew she was their last hope—the only being capable of restoring balance. But Zalarak was relentless; he had spies lurking in every shadow, seeking out those who dared defy him. If he discovered anyone aiding Aurora, he unleashed his wrath—destroying families, villages, and entire communities without mercy. His hatred for Aurora burned fiercely, for she was the sole threat to his dominion. Desperate to end her before she could awaken her full power, Zalarak's hunt intensified, his every move calculated to snuff out the light and plunge Etheria into eternal darkness. Yet, amidst the fear and destruction, hope endured, carried by those who believed in Aurora's destiny to rise.

Tessa revealed, "Clara, Victor, and Elias have been captured by Zalarak's forces. They have hidden them somewhere, and only you can find them, Aurora." Hearing this, Aurora's heart raced, but a glimmer of hope ignited within her—at least they were alive. She responded firmly, "Yes, but Elias met me before and warned me about these evil forces. Where should I search for them?" Aurora paused, her thoughts gaining clarity. "I understand now— whenever the dark forces sense someone aiding me, they tear them away, believing it will weaken me. But they are wrong. I am as strong as ever. I carry the love of Clara and Victor, and they are not just my guardians—they are parents too. Their love fuels my resolve."

Aurora sat up, gripping the edges of her blanket. She recalled Tessa's explanation: her parents had not been ordinary beings. They had been protectors of Etheria, powerful entities who had ruled with wisdom and grace.

Her mother, Queen Elara, had been a beacon of light, her divine energy unmatched. When Zalarak attacked the kingdom, Elara had just given birth to Aurora. Weakened from childbirth, Elara had sacrificed her remaining strength, pouring every ounce of her power into Aurora. It was a final act of love and hope.

Magnus, Aurora's father, had been killed by Zalarak. Stricken with grief over the loss of Elara, Aurora's Father, he had still fought valiantly to protect Etheria and his family. But Zalarak, driven by treachery and bolstered by his vast army, had betrayed and overwhelmed him. With King Magnus gone, Etheria was left without a ruler, relying solely on its wise Gurus and loyal guardians to maintain balance across the realms. Among them was Guru Altheron, the eldest and most revered of the Etherian council, who now bore the heavy responsibility of guiding and protecting the kingdom in these perilous times.

Aurora felt tears streaming down her face, both from grief and a sense of immense responsibility.

Tessa's words played over in her mind:

"You are the glory of Etheria, Aurora. Our ancestors declared it so. But you must walk your own path to spread the light across all realms."

Aurora closed her eyes, trying to calm the storm inside her. She could feel the truth of Tessa's words resonating within her soul. She had always felt different, but now she knew why.

In the faint morning light filtering through her window, Aurora got up, walked to her desk, and opened her tarot deck. She shuffled the cards carefully, her thoughts a mix of hope and fear. She needed guidance, and this time, she trusted the universe to show her the way.

She drew three cards and laid them on the table:

The Emperor – Leadership, stability, and control.

This card spoke directly to Aurora's current challenges. It was a call to embrace her role as a leader—not only in her tech company but as the destined ruler of Etheria.

The Tower – Sudden change, upheaval, and revelation.

The Tower reminded her that chaos was part of the journey. Zalarak's threats, her struggles with investors, and her awakening were all part of the necessary upheaval before transformation.

The Star – Hope, inspiration, and divine guidance.

This card filled Aurora's heart with warmth. It was a reminder that she was not alone. Tessa,Guru Altheron, and the light of Etheria were guiding her.

As Aurora placed the cards back in the deck, she felt a shift within her. A faint, golden light seemed to emanate from her chest, warm and reassuring.

She walked to her window and looked at the sky, still dark with the remnants of the night. She whispered softly, "Tessa, I hear you. Magnus, Elara, I miss you. I promise to walk this path, no matter how difficult it gets."

Aurora didn't have all the answers yet, but she felt a clarity she hadn't experienced before. The light within her was growing stronger, and with it, her resolve.

"Zalarak may have power," she thought, "but he doesn't have what I do—love, light, and purpose. I will find a way to fulfill my destiny. Etheria will rise again."

With that thought, Aurora prepared for a new day, one step closer to becoming the bridge between realms that she was meant to be.

Chapter Seven: The Leap of Faith—Starting a Tech Company

The next day, as Aurora prepared for the office, she checked her email and was struck by a wave of disappointment. The big investors she had been counting on had sent rejection emails, declining to invest in her company, **Nova Lumina Technologies**. The news was accompanied by a string of cancellations from existing clients, citing concerns over the defaming rumors circulating about the company's products.

Aurora froze in shock, unable to comprehend how everything had unraveled so swiftly. The rejection and cancellations felt like the fulfillment of the ominous message from the Tower card—a collapse that would pave the way for rebuilding on a stronger foundation.

Her phone buzzed incessantly. The board members of Nova Lumina Technologies were calling her, demanding urgent action. Among them were: Rhea Malhotra, Head of Product Innovation. Damien Carter, Chief Marketing Strategist. Leena Shah, Operations Manager. Ethan Blake, Financial Advisor. Sophia Kim, Customer Relations Lead. Rajiv Mehra, Legal Consultant. Vivian Hart, PR and Media Specialist.

They were urging Aurora to act quickly to retain the trust of existing clients and to convince potential investors. The team needed her leadership now more than ever, but in that moment, Aurora felt overwhelmed. Her thoughts clouded with uncertainty and frustration, she took a deep breath, recognizing the need for clarity. After a pause, Aurora called for an emergency board meeting. She resolved to face the challenges head-on and strategize with her team to save the company. Though shaken, she reminded herself of Tessa's words and the strength she carried within. This was her Tower moment—a chance to rise stronger.

In the Board meeting, she asked every team member's opinion and asked to share their way of resolving this situation.

Analysis of the Situation

Aurora opened the meeting by addressing the current crisis:

Client Cancellations: Existing clients were worried about the reliability of the company due to the defaming rumors.

Investor Withdrawals: The rejection emails indicated a lack of confidence in the company's growth potential.

Root Cause Identification: Aurora identified lapses in communication, marketing, and competitor sabotage as the key issues.

She emphasized the need for a comprehensive, sustainable action plan to rebuild trust, credibility, and momentum.

Action Plan Components

Reputation Management & Crisis Control

Lead: Vivian Hart (PR Specialist) Immediately release a statement clarifying the false claims and showcasing the company's actual performance metrics. Partner with trusted media outlets to publish case studies and testimonials from satisfied clients. Leverage social media to promote transparency and directly address client concerns.

Client Retention Strategy

Lead: Sophia Kim (Customer Relations) Personally contact each existing client to assure them of product quality and provide proof of performance.

Offer temporary discounts or extended warranties to ease client concerns.

Host a live Q&A session with Aurora and the product innovation team to address any doubts.

Legal Action

Lead: Rajiv Mehra (Legal Consultant) Investigate the defamation campaign and identify the perpetrators. Send legal notices to parties involved in spreading false rumors. Prepare to file lawsuits if the damage continues.

Product Enhancement & Rebranding

Lead: Rhea Malhotra (Product Innovation) Conduct an internal review of all product lines to ensure they exceed market standards. Collaborate with university students for fresh ideas on improving product usability and innovation. Develop a rebranding campaign to showcase a stronger, more refined product line.

Investor Engagement

Lead: Damien Carter (Marketing Strategist) Create a detailed recovery roadmap to present to investors, demonstrating how the company will overcome this challenge. Schedule follow-up meetings with investors who declined and present a revamped strategy. Launch an investor confidence campaign, sharing endorsements from credible industry leaders.

Employee Morale & Team Building

Lead: Leena Shah (Operations) Address internal concerns among employees, ensuring transparency and building confidence in the company's recovery plan. Conduct team-building activities to strengthen unity.

Aurora proposed involving the students from the State University to bring in fresh perspectives. A brainstorming session was organized where students shared their innovative solutions.

Key Insights from Students:

Transparency & Data-Driven Approach: "Why not release a transparency report that details the company's achievements, ongoing projects, and future goals? Let the numbers speak for themselves."

— A Computer Science student.

Crowd-Sourced Campaign: "Create a campaign involving existing clients to share their positive experiences. Real voices are more powerful than advertisements."

— A Marketing student.

Focus on Community Building: "Why not involve your client base in product design feedback? It shows you care about their opinions and builds loyalty."

— A Sociology student.

Gamification of Marketing: "Develop a mini-app or game related to your product's industry to attract attention and generate buzz in a fun way."

— A Gaming and UX Design student.

Collaborate with Academia: "Create a partnership program with universities for research and innovation. It'll showcase your commitment to knowledge and growth."

— An Engineering student.

Each board member was assigned clear deliverables with deadlines. Weekly check-ins were scheduled to track progress, and Aurora promised to personally oversee each component to ensure alignment with the company's vision.

As the meeting ended, Aurora emphasized the importance of resilience and collaboration. She thanked her team and the students for their input, reminding everyone that challenges often precede growth. With renewed determination, the team set out to implement the action plan.

Over the course of a grueling month, Aurora poured her energy into re-establishing her company, **Nova Lumina Technologies**, while battling personal and professional challenges. She was driven by a singular focus: to rebuild the brand's reputation and make it stronger than ever.

1. Reconnecting with Investors

Aurora scheduled back-to-back meetings with the investors who had initially rejected her proposals. Armed with a revamped business strategy, she approached them with clarity and passion.

Transparent Presentations: She outlined the steps Nova Lumina Technology had taken to address the crisis, such as improving product quality, hiring expert consultants, and creating a roadmap for recovery.

Incentive-Driven Investment Offers: Aurora introduced new benefits for investors, including equity options and additional profit-sharing opportunities once the company stabilized.

Demonstrating Value: With a portfolio of enhanced products, Aurora emphasized Nova Lumina Technology's focus on long-term sustainability, leveraging data from pilot runs to showcase better performance metrics.

Her sincerity, combined with the solid evidence of improvements, managed to convince a few investors to reconsider. These small victories gave her hope and momentum.

2. Winning Back Clients

To retain existing clients and attract new ones, Aurora launched a client-centric campaign:

Cheaper Rates, Better Services: She personally contacted clients, offering revised rates with added services to ensure their continued loyalty. For new clients, she positioned Nova Lumina Technology as a cost-effective yet innovative solution, appealing to smaller businesses and start-ups.

Personalized Client Support: Dedicated account managers were assigned to major clients to ensure seamless communication. Customized product demonstrations were provided to address client-specific needs. This hands-on approach started paying off, as many clients appreciated the transparency and renewed focus on customer satisfaction.

3. Collaborations with Trusted Institutions

Understanding the importance of aligning with reputable partners, Aurora forged collaborations with academic institutions and research organizations.

Mutual Growth Agreements: Nova Lumina offered internships, workshops, and technology seminars to foster talent while gaining fresh insights.

Resource Sharing: Institutions gained access to Nova Lumina's technology for research, while the company benefited from their intellectual resources.

This partnership not only boosted the company's credibility but also allowed for innovative breakthroughs, as young minds brought fresh perspectives.

4. Hiring Talented Students

From her meetings with State University students, Aurora identified exceptional talent and brought them on board:

Roles in Quality and Research: She hired students who showcased creativity and critical thinking in their suggestions. Their energy and enthusiasm revitalized the team, inspiring innovation in product development.

An Inclusive Culture: Aurora ensured these hires felt empowered and involved in key decisions, integrating them seamlessly into Nova Lumina's culture.

5. Guiding Herself with Tarot Cards

Despite her outward focus, Aurora continually turned to her trusted tarot deck for internal clarity.

Daily Draws for Guidance: Each morning, she drew a card for insight on her decisions. **The cards** often encouraged her to trust her intuition and remain resilient despite challenges.

The Star Card: One memorable day, she pulled **The Star**, symbolizing hope and renewal. This motivated her to keep pushing forward, even during moments of despair.

Shadow Work: **The Moon** card appeared during particularly stressful times, reminding Aurora to confront her fears and uncertainties rather than suppress them.

6. Personal Sacrifices

During this phase, Aurora neglected her personal well-being:

Sleepless Nights: Late-night meetings with investors, early-morning strategy sessions, and constant brainstorming left her physically drained.

Skipping Meals: She often skipped meals, prioritizing work over her health, which started to show in her weakening stamina.

Mental Fatigue: Balancing the immense pressure from clients, investors, and her team took a toll on her emotional state.

Yet, despite the challenges, she remained steadfast, drawing strength from her vision and the support of her team.

7. Execution of the Action Plan

The action plan was implemented step by step:

Vivian Hart successfully ran a PR campaign to counter the defamation, publishing factual articles and client testimonials. Sophia Kim regained trust with existing clients, securing reinstated orders. Rhea Malhotra introduced product updates that garnered attention from industry insiders. Damien Carter secured follow-up meetings with potential investors, with Aurora presenting the revised plans personally. Rajiv Mehra pursued legal action against the perpetrators of the defamation campaign, sending a strong message.

By the end of the month, Nova Lumina Technologies began seeing signs of recovery: A few major clients renewed their contracts. Positive press started shifting public perception. New investors showed interest, with one major backer agreeing to fund future innovations.

Though the journey ahead was still challenging, Aurora's resilience, strategic thinking, and the collective effort of her team provided a solid foundation for the company's revival.

In her quiet moments, she reflected on how each tarot card and dream encounter had subtly guided her actions. It was as though the universe was aligning her steps toward not only rebuilding Nova Lumina but also discovering her greater purpose.

With her company, Nova Lumina Technologies, back on its feet, Aurora didn't stop at mere stabilization. She knew that to regain the trust of the market, she needed to do something bold and decisive.

Marketing Campaign:

Aurora launched a comprehensive campaign titled "Illuminate Tomorrow with Nova Lumina", focusing on transparency, innovation, and reliability.

Social media platforms were flooded with customer testimonials and video demonstrations of Nova Lumina's cutting-edge tech. Collaboration announcements with esteemed academic institutions and research labs were made public. Ads highlighted the affordability and value of Nova Lumina's products for businesses of all sizes.

Press Conference: At the heart of the campaign was a high-profile press conference. Aurora confidently addressed the controversies surrounding her company, debunking false claims and showcasing her team's hard work to rebuild trust. She announced new deals, partnerships, and product launches, ensuring the audience of her commitment to innovation and excellence. Questions from journalists about her struggles were met with poise, further solidifying her image as a resilient leader.

The campaign was a success. Trust began to return, and Aurora's company gained positive traction in the market.

Though her business was regaining momentum, Aurora couldn't ignore the pull of her greater destiny. That night, as exhaustion and clarity danced within her mind, she called for Tessa in her dreams.

Tessa appeared, radiating wisdom and warmth. Aurora wasted no time and asked, "What must I do next to face Zalarak and his forces?"

Tessa's Advice: Tessa told her, "Aurora, the next step is to go within. You must retreat to a silent place where you can learn the energy systems deeply. This will prepare you to anticipate and counter every move of the dark forces."

Aurora needed to dedicate a full year to mastering the intricate balance of energies that govern all realms. The practice required a secluded environment where no one could disturb her focus. Tessa emphasized, "This is not just a preparation—it is the unlocking of your full potential, a gateway to becoming the leader of light."

As Aurora processed this, she asked a question that had been gnawing at her heart: "Why are you helping me so much, Tessa? Who are you to me?"

Tessa's expression softened as she revealed the truth:

"Aurora, I am your maternal grandmother. When you were just a three-month-old baby, Zalarak unleashed his wrath upon our family, determined to extinguish the light you carried. Your parents fought bravely to protect you, but I knew his dark forces were too powerful to hold back forever. That night, under the silver glow of a full moon, I used every ounce of my magic to charge a crystal locket with the purest light of Etheria—the light of truth, courage, and protection. This locket was more than just a shield; it was imbued with the energy to guide you toward your destiny."

Tessa paused, her eyes glistening with both pride and sorrow. "I placed the crystal locket on a sacred thread around your neck and wove an incantation into it, creating a seal that Zalarak's darkness could not penetrate. It was this seal that concealed your essence and protected you from his sight for 21 years. But it wasn't just the locket—it was the tarot deck too, an ancient tool to awaken your inner wisdom when the time was right."

Her voice softened as she spoke of Clara and Victor. "I saw the purity in their hearts, the strength of their love, and the simplicity of their lives. That's why I guided them to find you in the village garden. You were meant to live away from the chaos of Etheria, to grow in a world untouched by its burdens. It was essential for you to build resilience and wisdom, Aurora. This was not just my decision—it was the will of the universe."

Tessa placed a hand on Aurora's shoulder, her voice steady with purpose. "I may have protected you when you were a baby, but the time has come for you to protect yourself—and Etheria. The light in you is far greater than even I can understand. Use it wisely."

Tessa was a leader of the **Council of Gurus**, the ancient protectors and keepers of Etheria's wisdom.

Tessa's life in Etheria spanned thousands of years, during which she contributed to maintaining the balance of energies across realms. She specialized in understanding the universe's energy systems and using tools like tarot to guide and foresee the flow of life.

"Tarot has always been my best friend," Tessa said, her eyes gleaming with fondness. "Each deck I possess is charged with specific purposes. And you, Aurora, are more capable than you know. You can surpass me, but first, you must unlock your powers."

Aurora accepted the challenge. She agreed to create a secluded retreat where she could dedicate herself to the intense learning Tessa had described. But her heart ached to learn more about her grandmother's life, the history of her parents—**King Magnus** and **Queen Elara**—and how Etheria's fate was intertwined with her own. Tessa, however, gently stopped her. "There is more to tell, but it will come in due time. Focus now on your preparation. You will need it for the battles to come." **A**urora woke before dawn, her mind brimming with thoughts. She could feel a growing strength within her—a light that seemed to glow brighter with each revelation.

Determined, she began planning her retreat. She entrusted Nova Lumina Technology to her capable board and team, confident they could handle the company in her absence. As she envisioned the path ahead, she knew the time had come to fully embrace her role as the beacon of light that Etheria needed.

This wasn't just about defeating Zalarak; it was about leading all realms toward balance and harmony. The journey had only begun, but Aurora was ready to take the first steps toward her destiny.

Aurora, now equipped with a deeper understanding of energy fields, knew she needed to dedicate herself entirely to mastering the control of these forces. This was her next step toward preparing for the ultimate confrontation with Zalarak.

In a formal board meeting at Nova Lumina Technologies, Aurora addressed her team with a mix of confidence and vulnerability.

Her Message to the Team:

"I want to share with you all an important decision. I will be taking a leave of absence for one year. This company has been my dream, and together, we've built a foundation strong enough to stand the test of time. Now, I trust you, my team, to carry forward this vision in my physical absence."

She assured them she would remain accessible for guidance remotely, but her focus would be elsewhere.

"Our core values of integrity, innovation, and delivering value to our clients must remain non-negotiable, no matter

what challenges arise. Whether we face profit or loss, the promise we made to our clients must be upheld. This is how we differentiate ourselves in this competitive market."

The board members were supportive. They admired her vision and trusted her leadership, even from afar.

Investors were reassured by the steady profits and stability Aurora had established.

Clients, now satisfied with Nova Lumina's reliable services and innovative products, were expected to continue their loyalty.

Among those present was **Ryan**, the company's lead developer.

Ryan was a talented programmer and a key figure in Nova Lumina Technology's growth. However, his ambition was laced with greed.

Upon hearing Aurora's announcement, Ryan saw an opportunity to exploit her absence. In his mind, he began scheming to create a separate deal with one of the company's largest clients, intending to siphon resources and launch a competing venture.

To everyone else, Ryan appeared enthusiastic and supportive, but his true intentions were far from loyal.

Aurora, deeply focused on her spiritual and physical preparation, had no idea of Ryan's growing betrayal.

Chapter Eight: The Island of Solace

Aurora had recently purchased a private island—a serene and secluded haven perfect for her practices.

This decision came after years of successful ventures, savvy investments, and connections in high society that gave her access to rare opportunities.

The island was untouched by the chaos of urban life, surrounded by lush greenery, sparkling blue waters, and natural energy that resonated with Aurora's soul.

Aurora's island was a place of solitude, simplicity, and deep connection to herself and the universe. The space was carefully designed to foster her growth, both spiritually and intellectually, as she prepared for the battle that lay ahead.

Her living space was minimal, with only the essentials to support her journey. A small tech room was tucked away in one corner, equipped with the necessary tools to stay connected to her business. Here, she could monitor the activities of her company and interact only with her board members, staying aware of the ongoing situation while remaining physically removed from the business. This was her lifeline to the world she had built, though she only allowed herself to communicate when absolutely necessary.

The meditation hall was the heart of the island, where she could delve deep into her practices. It was adorned with Tarot cards, candles, and herbs that filled the room with a peaceful, calming energy. Shelves lined the walls, holding countless books—both spiritual and intellectual—each one a piece of her quest for understanding. This room was where Aurora would spend hours in reflection, seeking guidance from the universe and preparing herself for the challenges ahead.

Her bedroom was simple, almost ascetic with Crystal ball gifted by Jonathan. Aurora had made the choice to sleep on the earth instead of a bed, believing that connecting directly with the natural world would deepen her sense of grounding and alignment. The open space around her room was expansive, providing room for her many interests, from painting to stargazing, to simply walking barefoot on the soil to reconnect with the energy of the earth.

The small kitchen was tucked away but essential to her lifestyle. Here, Aurora cooked her own meals, drawing sustenance not just from the food, but from the act of self-reliance. She believed that nourishing her body through the process of preparing food with her own hands would strengthen her in ways beyond physical sustenance.

This island was more than a sanctuary—it was a sacred space, safeguarded by Tessa's powerful spellwork to shield Aurora from the reach of evil forces. However, on every new moon night, the protective magic weakened, leaving the island vulnerable. During these nights, a special contingent of Etherian forces silently guarded Aurora, ensuring her safety. Unaware of this secret protection, Aurora embraced the island as her refuge, a crucible where she could heal, learn, and grow—physically, emotionally, and spiritually. It became the place where she honed her essence, preparing for the monumental battles and enlightenment that lay ahead.

As Aurora prepared to leave for her retreat, she called a final team meeting.

She reiterated her faith in her team and reminded them of their shared responsibility to uphold Nova Lumina's legacy.

She left Ryan, as lead developer, with the responsibility of overseeing the technical operations, unknowingly placing him in a position of trust he did not deserve.

Aurora left the meeting feeling at peace, ready to begin her journey on the island. She understood that her spiritual growth was now just as vital as her professional success.

The First Night on the Island, When Aurora arrived on the island, she felt a deep sense of calm. She stood barefoot on the sandy shore, breathing in the salty air and listening to the rhythmic crashing of waves. For the first time in months, her mind was still.

She silently called out to Tessa in her thoughts:

"I'm here, ready to learn, ready to grow, ready to fight."

As she meditated that night, the stars above seemed to shimmer with a message of hope. Aurora felt an overwhelming sense of strength, as if the universe itself were aligning in her favor.

Little did she know, while she was entering a period of profound transformation, forces within her company were conspiring against her. The battle was not just for Etheria but also for the empire she had built in the mortal world.

In the stillness of the night, as Aurora slept, Tessa appeared once again in her dreams, her presence gentle yet commanding. She spoke with calm authority, guiding Aurora to create a disciplined routine that would help her prepare for the great journey ahead, both spiritually and mentally.

Tessa instructed Aurora, "You must align yourself with the rhythm of the universe, harmonize with nature, and sharpen your senses. To do so, you must follow a daily schedule, one that connects you to the divine and strengthens your inner power."

The schedule Tessa outlined was simple but intense, a path of deep transformation:

Morning Routine:

• 4:00 AM – Wake Up: Begin your day early, when the world is still in slumber. This is the time of peace and clarity, when the veil between worlds is thinnest.

• 4:00 AM - 6:00 AM – Meditation: Dedicate these first two hours to deep meditation. Clear your mind, connect to your soul, and invite the wisdom of the universe to guide you. Let your mind quiet and prepare for the day ahead.

• 6:00 AM – 7:00 AM – Yoga: Engage in yoga to awaken your body. Stretch, open, and energize your muscles, allowing the physical to align with the spiritual.

• 7:00 AM – 8:00 AM – Clean Your Space: Take time to clean your surroundings. A clean environment creates clarity within. Make your space sacred, for it reflects the purity of your soul.

•	8:00 AM – 9:00 AM – Prepare Food: Prepare a simple, wholesome vegetarian meal. Let this act nourish your body, mind, and spirit. The food you eat should sustain you as you walk the path ahead.

Daytime:

•	9:00 AM - 11:00 AM – Office Time: You will dedicate these two hours to your company. Stay connected with your board members, monitor progress, and manage the tasks that need your attention. This is your responsibility to the world you have built.

•	11:00 AM - 4:00 PM – Study and Reflection: Spend 4-5 hours reading and learning. Seek knowledge that will help you understand the workings of the universe and the energies that surround you. Engage with books, scrolls, and wisdom that will prepare you for the battle ahead.

•	4:00 PM - 5:00 PM – Gardening & Nature Walk: Go outside and connect with the land. Garden, plant, and nurture life. Spend time in the jungle of your island, observing the plants, animals, and the natural rhythms around you. This will sharpen your senses and ground you in the reality of the earth.

Evening Routine:

•	5:00 PM - 7:00 PM – Painting and Creativity: Allow yourself to create freely, whether through painting, sketching, or any form of artistic expression. This will help you connect to your inner creativity, which is vital for both spiritual and practical purposes.

- 7:00 PM - 8:00 PM – Meditation: As the day draws to a close, meditate once more. Let go of any stresses and align yourself with the divine energies you've worked with throughout the day. This practice will help you settle into your peaceful state before rest.

- 8:00 PM – 9:00 PM – Eat: Keep your evening meal simple and nourishing, but do not eat after 6:00 PM. This time is for spiritual reflection, not for indulging the body.

General Principles:

- Vegetarian Diet: Your body must be treated with respect, so consume only vegetarian food to keep your energy clear and aligned.

- Nature Time: Spend significant time with nature. Observe it with mindfulness—how the trees sway, how the animals behave, how the weather shifts. Let these observations sharpen your senses, and in turn, sharpen your mind.

- Silence and Solitude: In the jungle, away from the built-up space, you must observe the natural world without distractions. Listen to the whispers of nature. Become one with the land.

Tessa smiled as Aurora absorbed the guidance. "This path will not be easy, but it will strengthen you. Through this schedule, you will learn discipline, balance, and connection to the energies that flow through the universe. It will prepare you to face the darkness that lies ahead, and unlock the power within you."

As Tessa's image began to fade, Aurora woke up, her mind buzzing with the clarity of the vision. She knew that following this schedule would require discipline, but she was ready. This was her path to enlightenment, to uncovering her true self and becoming the beacon of light the universe had destined her to be.

For three months, Aurora faithfully followed the routine Tessa had laid out for her. The transformation was gradual but powerful, and the changes were undeniable. Her senses had sharpened to a degree she had never imagined. She could hear the faintest rustle of leaves and the distant calls of animals, understanding their language as if they spoke directly to her soul. She could sense the flow of the elements—earth, water, fire, air, and space—intertwining with her being. She began to perceive the interconnectedness of all things: how the elements and energies flowed seamlessly through nature and into her, as though her small identity was merely a drop in an ocean of infinite existence.

Through her readings of ancient scriptures and mystical texts, Aurora came to understand a profound truth: Everything is connected. The separation we feel is merely an illusion created by our limited identities. The world, the universe, and every living being are bound together by an invisible thread. She realized that her work was not just to fight the darkness but to reconnect the pieces of the puzzle, to restore balance between all realms, and to bridge the light that had been dimmed by forces like Zalarak.

Aurora began to modify her routine to deepen her practice. She intensified her meditation sessions, spending hours in stillness, exploring her consciousness and feeling the pulse of the universe. The more she delved within, the more she discovered about her soul's capabilities. The silence became her teacher, and she learned to move through time and space with ease, seeing visions of other realms and receiving guidance from ancient wisdom.

Despite the profound growth, Aurora faced many difficulties. The physical strain of her new lifestyle often left her in pain—her body ached from the constant manual labor, and the healing nature of the island did little to alleviate the soreness of her muscles. The insects of the jungle, too, were relentless, and she was frequently bitten by mosquitoes and other creatures. At first, she was fearful of the snakes, jaguars, and other jungle animals that roamed freely around her. But over time, Aurora began to recognize the sacredness of these beings and their role in the natural balance. She stopped seeing them as threats and began to see them as teachers, guides, and protectors of the land.

With her growing connection to nature, Aurora learned the art of self-healing. She collected herbs from the jungle, crafted ointments, and made medicines from the plants that grew around her. The jungle's bounty was her ally, and she understood its ability to heal both the body and the spirit. Whenever she faced physical pain, she would apply these healing remedies and, in time, the discomfort subsided, leaving her feeling stronger and more attuned to the energy of the earth.

Every night, Tessa appeared in her dreams, offering guidance and wisdom to Aurora. Her presence was comforting, and she reminded Aurora of the lessons she had to learn and the challenges that lay ahead. But Tessa always emphasized that the ultimate work—Aurora's transformation, her spiritual evolution, and the overcoming of the darkness—was something only Aurora could achieve through her own efforts. Tessa was there to guide, but the path was Aurora's to walk.

Aurora also found joy in the simple moments of life on the island. She often spent time by the river, playing with the fish and water creatures, letting the cool water refresh her spirit. The jungle, with all its vibrancy and life, became her sanctuary. The sounds of the animals, the rustle of the trees, the whisper of the wind through the leaves—it all felt like music to her soul. She had found heaven on earth in this secluded paradise.

Her training intensified, as Aurora knew her time for greater challenges was approaching. Her connection to the natural world deepened, and she continued to hone her abilities, learning how to manipulate energy and interact with the elements. As the weeks turned into months, her mastery over her body and spirit grew stronger, but so did the understanding that her battle was far from over.

The stillness of the island allowed her to prepare, physically and mentally, for the larger confrontation that awaited her. Every step she took, every lesson she learned, was part of the process of becoming the leader Etheria needed— someone capable of facing Zalarak and restoring balance to all the realms. And through it all, she knew she was never truly alone. The jungle, the elements, Tessa, and the energy of the universe itself were guiding her every step of the way.

Eleven months had passed since Aurora began her intense spiritual training on the island, and she had emerged completely transformed. Her physical appearance was radiant, almost ageless, with a glow that reflected the deep rejuvenation of her soul. Her once-tired eyes were now filled with clarity and purpose. She felt lighter, more powerful, and deeply connected to the universe around her. The meditation, yoga, and immersion in the elements had brought her closer to her higher self than ever before. She was not just physically stronger but spiritually elevated, with a newfound mastery over her energy and senses.

On the ominous night of the new moon, the island's serene tranquility was shattered. Zalarak, the dark master of shadow and chaos, had discovered Aurora's hidden sanctuary. His power peaked in the absence of light, and Tessa's magical protection, weakened under the new moon, left Aurora vulnerable. As Aurora slept soundly, bathed in the radiant glow of the crystal ball, Zalarak began his sinister plan.

On the night of the new moon, an unexpected mystical eclipse descended upon the island, shrouding it in an unnatural darkness. This rare, ancient event, foretold to occur once every century, aligned with the natural cycles of the world to dampen all sources of magical light. The crystal ball, usually a beacon of radiant energy, dimmed to a faint glow, its protective aura faltering against the cosmic phenomenon.

Sensing this moment of vulnerability, Zalarak seized the opportunity. With a flick of his hand, a black cloth of impenetrable darkness materialized, wrapping itself around the crystal ball. The faint glow was extinguished instantly, plunging the room into an eerie stillness. The warmth and safety of the crystal's light were replaced by an oppressive cold, as if the very essence of the room had been drained.

Zalarak's presence filled the space like a suffocating shadow, the air thick and heavy with the weight of his dark energy. This was the moment he had been waiting for—a confluence of celestial events and his own cunning, granting him access to Aurora's sanctuary.

Before Aurora could awaken, Zalarak captured her with ease, binding her in tendrils of shadow energy that sapped her strength. He sneered, his deep voice dripping with malice. "Did you think you could escape me forever, child of light? I will end your lineage tonight and bring eternal darkness to Etheria."

Just as all seemed lost, a powerful surge of light erupted into the room, shattering the oppressive shadows. Kael appeared, radiating golden energy that cut through the darkness like a blade. With unwavering determination, he faced Zalarak.

"You will not harm her," Kael declared, his voice a steady force that reverberated through the space. "Your reign of terror ends here."

Zalarak roared in fury and launched a series of vicious attacks, but Kael countered each one with precision and strength. Their battle was fierce, the room glowing with bursts of dark and light energy. Finally, Kael unleashed a wave of blinding golden chains that bound Zalarak, rendering him powerless.

Aurora, freed from the shadows, watched in awe and gratitude as Kael subdued the dark force that had haunted her for so long. Though shaken, she knew this was a sign— her battle with Zalarak was far from over, but she was not alone.

The encounter solidified Aurora's decision to leave the island and return to the city. She would balance her time between her business and her spiritual practices, continuing her mission to spread light and awaken others. The battle had just begun, and she was ready to fight, armed with newfound resolve and a powerful ally by her side.

After the intense battle with Zalarak, Aurora sat in her meditation hall, nursing her wounds. Her body ached, but her spirit remained unbroken. She reflected deeply on the fight, replaying each moment in her mind. The battle had revealed a harsh truth—Zalarak wasn't just powerful; he was cunning, exploiting weaknesses she hadn't even realized she had. His attacks had targeted not only her body but also her mind, striking when her focus wavered.

Aurora's fast-healing ability worked like a miracle, and within days, her physical injuries were gone. Yet, the unanswered questions lingered—*Why had I failed? What more do I need to learn?*

That night, as she drifted into restless sleep, Tessa appeared in her dream. Her expression was grave as she shared the hidden truth. "Aurora, the timing of Zalarak's attack was no coincidence. It was a new moon night—the one time my protective spells over the island weaken. Somehow, Zalarak discovered this secret and used it to breach the island's defenses. This is why he struck when he did."

Aurora listened intently, but Tessa's tone grew more uncertain. "There is another mystery. Someone else was protecting you during the battle—a force I did not summon, someone whose presence I cannot trace. I am searching for this unknown ally, for their power was extraordinary, and their intent seemed to align with yours."

The revelation left Aurora thoughtful. Who was this protector? And why had they come to her aid at such a critical moment? While she felt gratitude for their intervention, she knew she couldn't rely on unknown help in the future. Her failure had illuminated gaps in her preparation, and she resolved to confront them.

The encounter had been a harsh lesson, but Aurora knew that growth often came through struggle. She was determined to rise stronger, more focused, and ready for whatever challenges lay ahead.

Next night, as Aurora meditated to seek clarity, Tessa appeared in her dream, her presence radiant and soothing.

"Aurora, Zalarak is a dark force fueled by ego and greed," Tessa explained. "Ego thrives on division, on fear, and on illusions of power. You can never defeat him through force alone. The only way to truly overpower Zalarak is **through complete surrender**—not to him, but to the infinite source of light and balance. You must learn to embody the **zero state of being**, where the ego dissolves, and you become a vessel of universal harmony. In that state, no darkness can touch you."

Tessa continued, her voice filled with ancient wisdom, "Zalarak is not the only dark force. The **universe operates on a balance of dualities**—light and dark, creation and destruction. Just as Zalarak wields dark energies, there are others aligned with his power. But equally, there are forces of light, pure and divine, waiting for you to call upon them."

Forces of Darkness and Light

Tessa revealed the names of the forces that shaped the balance of the cosmos.

Dark Forces: Zalarak: The Lord of Evil Ego and Division. Noxira: Mistress of Shadows, weaving fear and deceit. Oblivar: The Void Bringer, who thrives on despair and hopelessness. Malegor: The Firestorm of Anger and Wrath. Xeraphus: The Whisperer of Doubt and Betrayal.

Light Forces: Lumina: Guardian of Purity and Clarity. Solara: The Radiant Flame of Courage and Strength. Aetherion: Keeper of Knowledge and Wisdom. Zephyra: Bringer of Calm Winds and Peace. Celestara: Weaver of Hope and Renewal.

Tessa urged Aurora to forge alliances with the light forces. "Call out to them, Aurora. Meditate on their energies, learn their essence, and invite them to be with you. They will not only fight by your side but also aid you in healing and wisdom. In the next battle, you will not stand alone if you open your heart to them."

Aurora listened intently. "How do I reach them, Grandmother?" she asked.

"You already have the key," Tessa replied with a smile. "Your meditation, your surrender, your purity of purpose—all of these open the gateway to their realms. Go deeper, seek them, and they will come to you."

When Aurora awoke, she felt a renewed sense of purpose. She spent days in intense meditation, visualizing the energies of Lumina, Solara, Aetherion, Zephyra, and Celestara. She studied their qualities and felt their presence growing stronger in her life.

She also dedicated herself to creating a deeper bond with nature and the elements, understanding how to channel their power in alignment with the universal balance.

Her resolve was firm. The next time Zalarak come for her, she would not stand alone. She would be a vessel for the forces of light, a beacon of hope and harmony in the face of darkness. **This was her destiny—to restore the balance in Etheria and beyond.**

Aurora spent her final days on the island in deep meditation, aligning herself with the divine forces of light that she had called upon. The energies of **Lumina, Solara, Aetherion, Zephyra,** and **Celestara** infused her being, blessing her with inner strength, clarity, and purpose. She could feel their presence surrounding her, like an unshakable shield of light.

"Remember, Aurora," Lumina's voice echoed in her meditative state, "we are always with you. Call upon us when you need strength, guidance, or healing. You are ready to step into the world and spread the light."

Aurora opened her eyes, her spirit ablaze with newfound power and serenity. She decided that her return to the city and her office would be unannounced—a surprise to everyone. She wanted her presence to speak louder than words.

Chapter Nine: Aurora's Miraculous Reflection

The day came for her departure. Aurora left her island sanctuary and traveled back to the bustling city. As she stepped into her office building, her transformation was undeniable.

Aurora was radiant, her presence almost ethereal. Her skin glowed with a divine light, her smile exuded warmth and serenity, and her eyes sparkled with wisdom and power. Every person she passed in the corridors turned to look at her, their expressions a mix of awe and admiration. Her energy was magnetic—calm yet commanding, soothing yet invigorating.

The air seemed lighter, charged with positivity, as if her very presence had shifted the energy of the entire space. Employees whispered among themselves, captivated by her miraculous transformation. Some felt a sense of peace wash over them just by being in her vicinity.

Aurora walked gracefully to the boardroom, her aura drawing everyone toward her like moths to a flame.

Once inside the boardroom, Aurora turned to her team, her voice calm but commanding. "I'd like everyone to join me here," she said with a radiant smile. Within moments, all the board members and department heads were seated, eager and curious about what she had to share.

Aurora began by addressing the company's current state. She listened intently as each member gave updates about the progress and challenges during her absence. She nodded, acknowledging their efforts, and then one of the board members, **Andrew**, broke the silence.

"Aurora, we're thrilled to have you back, but we must ask... how has this transformation happened? You're... different. It's as if you've brought the divine into this very room," he said, his voice filled with genuine admiration and curiosity.

Aurora smiled, her gaze steady. "Thank you, Andrew, and thank you all for your dedication during my time away. What you see is the result of surrender, self-discovery, and alignment with the universal energies that guide all life. It wasn't an easy journey, but it was necessary. I learned to connect deeply with my soul, to harness the power within, and to understand that true leadership comes from light, not control.

"And now," she continued, "I want to share something new. Alongside our core business goals, we will add a mission to empower every soul that seeks spiritual connection and divine guidance. We will create a platform to teach self-transformation for those who wish to explore it. This will not only be our unique offering but also our way of contributing to the world. Light is not meant to be contained; it must spread."

The room was silent for a moment, the weight of her words sinking in. Then, one by one, the board members began nodding. The energy in the room shifted; everyone felt inspired and uplifted.

"How do you plan to teach us, Aurora?" another board member asked.

Aurora's eyes sparkled. "I will guide those who are ready. Whether it's through workshops, meditative practices, or one-on-one sessions, I'll create opportunities for transformation. It won't be mandatory—it's a journey each person must choose for themselves. But for those willing to step into the light, I will be here to show the way."

The board erupted in applause, moved by her vision.

Aurora ended the meeting with a clear action plan for the business and the new initiative. As everyone left the room, they felt not just motivated but profoundly inspired. Many silently resolved to join her spiritual sessions, eager to learn from her wisdom and transformative journey.

For Aurora, this was the beginning of a new era—not just for her company but for the countless souls she hoped to uplift. **She was ready to lead the world into light, one step at a time.**

The next day, Aurora entered the boardroom, radiating her usual calm and grounded energy. The meeting started with updates, and midway through, **Andrew,** a senior board member, cleared his throat and addressed the group.

"We have an important issue to discuss," he said, glancing around the room. "Our lead developer, **Ryan,** attempted to compromise the company by negotiating a secret deal with one of our most important clients. However, we discovered his actions just in time, and he was detained before the deal could be finalized. He is now in legal custody."

A murmur spread through the room as the board members exchanged surprised and angry looks. All eyes turned to Aurora, anticipating her response.

Aurora remained serene, her face unreadable as she listened. When Andrew finished, she spoke in her usual composed tone.

"Thank you for bringing this to my attention. Here's what I would like you to do: arrange for Ryan's release immediately. I want to meet with him personally."

The room fell silent, stunned by her decision. Andrew hesitated. "Aurora, are you sure? His actions could have caused immense damage to the company. Shouldn't we take stricter action to set an example?"

Aurora smiled gently. "I understand your concerns, Andrew. But sometimes, the most profound example is forgiveness. Let me speak with him."

Later that day, Ryan stepped into Aurora's office, his posture tense and his face etched with the weight of his guilt. His eyes betrayed sleepless nights and an inner turmoil that seemed to war against his very soul. Aurora looked up from her desk, her warm yet discerning gaze meeting his. With a gentle nod, she gestured for him to sit.

"Ryan," she began softly, her voice a delicate balance of compassion and strength. "I want to understand—what led you to this? Why did you betray the trust we built?"

Ryan's lips twisted into an unsettling smirk, a shadow of arrogance flickering across his face. "Trust? Between us?" he scoffed, his voice dripping with venom. "The only trust I honor is with Zalarak. Do you really think you can stand against him alone? You're weak, Aurora... too weak to fight him."

A chilling laugh erupted from Ryan, his words striking Aurora like shards of ice. The very mention of Zalarak's name sent a shiver down her spine, but she steadied herself, her calm exterior unshaken. "How do you know Zalarak?" she asked, her voice measured. "Does your betrayal have anything to do with him?"

Ryan's laughter grew darker, more menacing. "Not just me," he sneered. "Every time you thought you were gaining ground, Zalarak was there to tear you down. Those who tried to help you? They all paid the price. Elias? Taken. Your parents? Disappeared. Even Jonathan—he wasn't on leave, Aurora. He's dead. And Joy," he added with a cruel chuckle. "You thought he loved you? You fool. He was Zalarak's pawn, sent to shatter your spirit."

Each word was a dagger aimed at her heart, but Aurora's intuition told her something deeper was at play. This wasn't the Ryan she knew. His words, vile as they were, seemed like echoes of another voice—one that didn't belong to him. She leaned forward slightly, her calm gaze piercing through the storm of his bitterness. "Thank you, Ryan," she said evenly. "Thank you for making every blurred picture so painfully clear."

Ryan's smug expression faltered as Aurora locked eyes with him. There was a radiant energy in her gaze, an unseen force that began to ripple through the room. Ryan's bravado crumbled as he staggered back, clutching his head. A guttural groan escaped his lips, and moments later, he collapsed into the chair.

When he finally spoke again, his voice was trembling, raw, and full of remorse. "Aurora... it wasn't me," he choked out. "Something dark—it's been controlling me, whispering to me, feeding my greed, my fears, my insecurities. I thought

I could handle it, that I could use it, but... I've been a puppet all along."

Aurora leaned closer, her voice steady but tender. "Ryan, darkness only controls what we allow it to. It preys on our wounds, our fears, and our weaknesses. But admitting the truth is your first step toward breaking free. That takes immense courage."

Ryan looked at her, his eyes brimming with tears. "Do you think I can ever be free of it? That I can come back from this?"

Aurora placed a hand over her heart, her voice radiating conviction. "I believe every soul has the capacity to rise, no matter how far it has fallen. Darkness doesn't define you, Ryan. You still have light within you. You just need to reclaim it."

Tears streamed freely down Ryan's face. "I don't deserve your forgiveness, Aurora. Not after everything I've done. I don't even deserve to be here."

Aurora's voice softened, yet her words carried a profound weight. "Forgiveness isn't about deserving, Ryan. It's about breaking the chains that bind us to pain—yours and mine. I forgive you because I believe in the light within you. But forgiveness doesn't erase the consequences. Trust must be rebuilt, step by step."

Ryan nodded, his voice thick with emotion. "I don't know if I can ever make this right, but I'll try, Aurora. I swear I'll try."

Aurora smiled, her gaze unwavering. "That's all I ask, Ryan. Redemption isn't easy, but it's worth every step. Remember, the light you seek isn't something outside—it's within you. Awaken it, and you'll find your way."

For the first time in what felt like forever, Ryan felt a flicker of hope ignite within him. The oppressive weight of his guilt began to lift, replaced by the steady glow of a soul ready to heal.

Word of Aurora's decision spread quickly through the office. Employees were astounded by her magnanimity, and whispers of admiration filled the halls. "She's like a goddess," one employee remarked. "Who else could forgive so easily and still inspire so much respect?"

Even in the industry, the story of Aurora's forgiveness reached other companies and clients. It was seen as a revolutionary act of leadership that embodied compassion and wisdom. People began to view her as more than just a successful entrepreneur—she was a beacon of light and inspiration.

During the next board meeting, Aurora addressed her team. "I understand that my decision to forgive Ryan might have surprised many of you," she began. "But I believe that forgiveness is one of the most powerful tools we have. It allows us to break the cycle of negativity and offer others a chance to redeem themselves. Our world is filled with mistakes, but it's also filled with opportunities to choose kindness and growth over punishment."

She paused, her serene gaze sweeping across the room. "If we, as leaders, cannot embody these values, how can we expect to create a better world? Forgiveness doesn't mean forgetting—it means choosing to see the potential for good in everyone."

The room erupted in applause. Aurora's words had struck a chord, inspiring everyone present to reflect on their own capacity for forgiveness and understanding.

Aurora's journey of transformation and success propelled her into extraordinary heights, establishing her as not only a billionaire but also a globally admired influencer. Her wealth was not merely a reflection of material abundance but a testament to her vision, resilience, and unparalleled ability to balance spirituality with business acumen.

The Grand Mansion

Aurora's primary residence was a breathtaking mansion situated on a sprawling estate near the edge of a serene lake. The mansion, designed to reflect both luxury and spirituality, featured: A meditation wing, complete with stained glass windows, serene water features, and an expansive library filled with ancient texts and modern works. A grand ballroom, often used for hosting charitable galas and spiritual workshops. An outdoor Zen garden, with intricate pathways, fountains, and sculptures symbolizing peace and balance. A private cinema and wellness spa, showcasing her balanced lifestyle of enjoyment and self-care. The mansion itself was powered by sustainable energy, showcasing Aurora's commitment to eco-conscious living.

Aurora's fleet of cars reflected her refined taste and penchant for innovation. She owned: A Rolls-Royce Phantom, customized with intricate celestial patterns on the interior. A Tesla Roadster, showcasing her support for clean energy. A Porsche 911 Turbo S, a nod to her appreciation for speed and elegance. A customized Range

Rover, used for her charity visits and trips to her remote island.

Aurora's portfolio of real estate spanned the globe: A villa in Bali, used for her personal retreats and spiritual workshops. A penthouse in New York City, designed as a hub for her international business meetings. A vineyard estate in Tuscany, reflecting her love for nature and fine living. Multiple properties in developing regions, dedicated to creating schools and shelters for underprivileged communities.

Aurora's philanthropy was a cornerstone of her legacy. She founded the Light of Hope Foundation, focusing on: Building schools in underserved areas, ensuring access to quality education for children worldwide. Empowering women through vocational training and mentorship programs. Supporting disaster relief efforts, providing aid and resources to affected communities.

Aurora's business ventures flourished under her leadership: Rising Stocks: Her company, AuroraTech, became a global leader in innovative solutions, with its stock value soaring. Collaborations: Aurora partnered with luxury brands, sustainable enterprises, and tech innovators, further solidifying her brand's global influence.

Aurora's generosity and connections with elite circles often led to an exchange of opulent gifts: She gifted a custom-designed diamond bracelet to a prominent investor during her company's anniversary celebration. She received a handcrafted harp from Ireland, symbolizing peace, from a spiritual leader. Luxury brands often sent her exclusive collections, knowing her influence could elevate their market presence.

Aurora often traveled on private luxury cruises, her favorite being a bespoke yacht designed for both leisure and reflection. These cruises often doubled as retreats, where she invited key clients, investors, and spiritual leaders for transformative experiences.

Her brand, Aurora's Light, gained a global presence with: Offices in 30+ countries. Products spanning technology, wellness, and education sectors. An online platform connecting millions worldwide to her teachings and brand initiatives.

Aurora's journey exemplified how material success and spiritual fulfillment could harmoniously coexist. She lived a life of purpose, creating ripples of positive change across the globe. Her wealth was not merely her own—it was a tool she used to uplift others, spread light, and leave an indelible mark on the world.

As time passed, Aurora continued to rise in her industry, her wealth and influence expanding across multiple sectors. She became a billionaire, with diverse streams of income from her tech company, investments, and new ventures. Yet, she remained grounded, dedicating her mornings to meditation in the serene space she had created in her grand mansion.

Aurora also launched her first book, **"The Billionaire Mystic: The Path Within,"** which chronicled her journey of transformation and offered guidance to others seeking spiritual awakening. The book became an instant bestseller, touching the hearts of millions.

She started teaching meditation for free, welcoming anyone willing to explore the depths of their soul. Her sessions became a sanctuary for those seeking clarity, healing, and connection. Aurora's vision of spreading light and empowering others was unfolding beautifully, one soul at a time.

Despite her immense success, Aurora remained humble and devoted to her purpose. She often reflected on her journey, knowing that her greatest battles—and triumphs—still lay ahead. **She was ready for them, shining brighter than ever.**

Aurora's success in the material world was unparalleled, but her heart was still drawn to Etheria, a land she had only glimpsed in her dreams and stories. Despite her achievements, she felt a longing to connect with her true purpose—to bring light and harmony to Etheria.

Chapter Ten: The Invitation to Etheria

One night, as Aurora meditated in her grand mansion, she summoned Tessa in her dreams. "Tessa," she asked, "when will I finally come to Etheria and see what is happening there?"

Tessa, radiant as ever, replied, "On your next birthday, I will come and take you to Etheria. Prepare yourself, my child."

Aurora's birthday was only five days away, and she began making preparations for her journey. Meanwhile, in Etheria, Tessa announced Aurora's arrival. The news spread like wildfire. The people of Etheria, filled with hope and joy, began decorating the realm with flowers, lights, and banners that read **"Welcome, Aurora—The Lightbearer."**

Zalarak, driven by vengeance, had escaped from Kael's fortified jail, slipping through the cracks of even the most powerful bindings. Now free, his wrath had no bounds. He had one goal: to eliminate Aurora and Kael, thereby seizing control over all the realms. "No one can save you now, Aurora," Zalarak hissed to himself, his voice dripping with malice. "Kael is occupied in another realm, unaware of my escape. After I destroy you, I'll deal with him and reign supreme across the dimensions", "I am waiting for the right time".

The news of Aurora's impending visit to Etheria reached Zalarak. Seething with rage and his usual cunning, he chose her birthday as the perfect moment to attack. "Her birthday," he sneered, "when she basks in her achievements and celebrates her vanity—it will be the ultimate irony to end her reign then."

Unaware of the storm brewing, Aurora was deeply immersed in her preparations for Etheria. She had designed a gown that reflected her journey—a dress crafted from shimmering pearls, each symbolizing a realm she had touched with her light and wisdom. The dress radiated ethereal beauty, a tangible representation of her inner transformation and the lives she had impacted.

As Aurora finalized her preparations, an unnatural silence descended upon her mansion. The air turned icy, and all sources of light—candles, lamps, even the faint glow of the moon—vanished as though devoured by an insatiable void. The darkness wasn't mere absence; it was alive, pulsing with malice.

From the shadows, Zalarak emerged, his form an amalgamation of seething darkness and malevolence. His laughter echoed like a sinister symphony, filling every corner of the room. "Aurora," he sneered, his voice dripping with mockery, "you've fought valiantly to reach this point. But did you truly believe you could escape me? You are alone, and this is the end of your defiance."

Aurora stood in the center of the room, her frame illuminated by an ethereal glow radiating from within her. She closed her eyes, letting her inner light expand, pushing back against the oppressive darkness. "You're wrong, Zalarak," she replied, her voice unwavering. "I am never alone. My light is eternal, untouchable by your shadows. And tonight, I will prove it."

With a guttural growl, Zalarak attacked, tendrils of darkness whipping toward her with the force of a hurricane. Aurora raised her hands, her light forming a shimmering barrier that absorbed the impact. Sparks of energy crackled and hissed as the opposing forces clashed.

Zalarak wasn't merely attacking—he was playing tricks, warping the room into a twisted labyrinth of illusions. Voices of doubt whispered in her ears, shadows formed into grotesque shapes, and memories of her past failures flashed before her eyes. But Aurora held her ground, her light burning brighter as she called upon the teachings of her ancestors. "Your tricks won't work, Zalarak," she said, her voice a beacon in the chaos. "I see through your darkness."

As the battle escalated, Aurora summoned her allies, the elemental forces of light. "Aetheria, Queen of Light, guide me! Luminor, Flame of Hope, strengthen me! Zephyra, Wind of Wisdom, unveil the truth! Aquarion, Healer of Depths, shield the innocent!"

One by one, the elemental energies answered her call, their radiant forms piercing through the darkness and surrounding Aurora in a halo of divine power. The clash of energies was deafening. Zalarak's darkness surged, consuming everything in its path, but Aurora countered with waves of blinding light, each infused with the combined strength of her allies and her unwavering spirit.

"Enough!" Zalarak roared, his voice shaking the very foundations of the mansion. He unleashed his most devastating attack, a vortex of pure malevolence meant to consume her entirely. Aurora closed her eyes, drew a deep breath, and focused every ounce of her energy into a single point within her. She whispered, "Light eternal, guide my hand."

The moment the vortex reached her, Aurora released a burst of energy so brilliant that it seemed to rip through the fabric of reality. The light engulfed Zalarak, forcing him to his knees. His form flickered, struggling against the radiant cage of light that now surrounded him.

Aurora stepped forward, her gaze steady and unyielding. "Your reign ends here, Zalarak," she declared, her voice echoing with the combined strength of her allies. "But I will not destroy you. The balance of the realms requires even darkness to exist. Instead, you will be imprisoned in Etheria, where your power will harm no one."

Zalarak's defiant glare faltered, replaced by a mix of fury and despair. The forces of light carried him away to Etheria's sacred prison, a realm designed to contain and neutralize darkness. His armies, leaderless and broken, scattered into the void.

As the first rays of dawn pierced through the dissipating darkness, Aurora stood victorious. The mansion, once a battlefield of despair, now shimmered with a tranquil light, a testament to the resilience of her spirit. Aurora's battle wasn't just a triumph of power—it was a triumph of the light within her, a reminder that even in the darkest hour, the light can never be extinguished.

Aurora's victory was met with widespread celebration. As she entered Etheria for the first time, the realm shone brighter than ever before. The people, the divine leaders, and the rulers of other realms gathered to honor her.

The festivities were grand, with music, dances, and speeches celebrating Aurora's wisdom, courage, and compassion. The kings and queens of the realms praised her decision to forgive and imprison Zalarak instead of destroying him, recognizing it as a testament to her understanding of universal balance.

Aurora, now the undisputed Lightbearer of Etheria and beyond, spoke to the gathered crowd:

"Victory is not in destroying your enemy but in transforming the darkness within and without. Together, we will ensure that balance prevails, and light continues to shine in all realms."

Aurora had learned the intricate balance between light and dark energies and, more importantly, how to neutralize evil forces by controlling their sources of power. She understood that Zalarak thrived in darkness, drawing his strength from the shadows that surrounded him. Determined to keep him subdued, she devised a clever strategy: large, luminous crystal spheres infused with divine energy were placed strategically along the walls of Zalarak's prison. These radiant crystals eliminated any dark spaces within the confinement, leaving Zalarak weakened and unable to recharge his sinister energies.

Trapped in perpetual light, Zalarak's powers dwindled to mere echoes of their former strength. His attempts to escape were futile, and his once-loyal forces, leaderless and disillusioned, scattered across the realms, fading into obscurity.

With Zalarak securely imprisoned and his influence extinguished, a new era of peace and unity dawned in Etheria. Aurora's leadership brought hope and healing to realms that had long been fractured by darkness. She became a bridge between Etheria and the material world, vowing to split her time between the two. Her mission was clear: to spread light and empowerment to all, inspiring every soul to awaken their inner strength and align with higher truths.

Aurora's journey had come full circle. She had overcome profound losses, faced her deepest fears, and embraced her destiny with courage and grace. Now, she stood as a beacon of hope—a living symbol of the harmony between material success and spiritual enlightenment. Her life was no longer just her own; it was a guiding force for all who sought the light, a testament to the power of transformation, and a reminder that even in the darkest times, light prevails.

The air in Etheria was electric with anticipation as Tessa announced Aurora as the new Queen of Etheria. The decision was met with cheers and celebrations that reverberated across the realm. Aurora, standing in the grand hall of Etheria's palace, felt a deep sense of honor and responsibility. She had not only won the trust of the people but had also proven herself worthy of leading a realm as mystical and vast as Etheria.

The coronation ceremony was magnificent. Leaders and emissaries from all realms gathered, dressed in their finest regalia, bringing offerings and gifts for their new queen. The Etherian crown, a masterpiece of ancient craftsmanship, was placed on Aurora's head by Tessa herself. It sparkled with the energy of the five elements—Earth, Water, Fire, Air, and Space—and pulsed with the unity of the divine forces.

Aurora, radiant in her pearl dress, stood tall, her aura exuding calm strength and divine grace. She vowed to uphold the balance of Etheria and ensure harmony across all realms.

Aurora's Coronation Speech: The grand hall of Etheria's palace was silent, yet the air buzzed with anticipation. Aurora, standing on the dais, radiated an aura of divine strength and grace. Her crown glimmered in harmony with her presence, embodying the balance of the five elements and the unity of realms. She raised her hand, signaling the gathering of leaders, kings, queens, and emissaries from across dimensions to lend her their ears.

With a serene yet commanding voice, she began:

"My beloved people of Etheria,

Leaders and guardians of realms,

And divine forces who grace us with your presence,

Today is not merely a day of celebration but a moment of reflection and purpose. I stand before you, humbled and honoured, as your queen—not to rule over you but to walk alongside you in our collective journey toward harmony.

The crown I wear is not a symbol of power; it is a reminder of my responsibility to uphold balance—balance between realms, between light and shadow, and, most importantly, between material and spiritual wealth.

Throughout my journey, I have walked the path of earthly success. I built an empire, achieved prosperity, and touched the heights of material abundance. Yet, it was in the stillness of my meditations, in surrendering to the flow of the universe, that I discovered the true essence of wealth.

Material wealth is necessary—it fuels progress, provides comfort, and creates opportunities for growth. But it must be guided by the principles of spiritual wisdom. Spiritual wealth, on the other hand, is the foundation of peace, purpose, and enlightenment. It teaches us to act with compassion, integrity, and respect for the balance of life.

When we pursue material success without spiritual grounding, we risk creating chaos. And when we seek spiritual enlightenment while neglecting our worldly responsibilities, we deny ourselves the opportunity to contribute to the physical world we inhabit. The two are not opposites; they are partners in the dance of creation.

As your queen, my vision is clear: Etheria will become the beacon of balance, a realm that demonstrates how material abundance can coexist with spiritual enlightenment.

We will create wealth that uplifts everyone, not just a few. We will foster wisdom that illuminates paths for generations to come. Let us ensure that our advancements in technology, trade, and knowledge serve to deepen our connection to the divine, the universe, and one another.

Forgiveness, Unity, and Healing: In this time of great transformation, let us remember the power of forgiveness. As I have learned through my trials, even the darkest forces have a purpose in the grand tapestry of life. Forgiveness does not excuse wrongdoing; it transforms it into an opportunity for growth. When we forgive, we break the chains of anger and ego, allowing us to rise above the limitations of fear and hatred.

Today, I call upon each of you—leaders, warriors, scholars, healers, and guardians—to join me in this mission.

Let us foster innovation with intention, ensuring that our creations heal rather than harm.

Let us teach our children not only the skills to thrive in the material world but also the wisdom to nurture their spirits.

Let us build bridges between realms, uniting the forces of light and shadow in service of the greater good.

I am not here to command; I am here to serve. And in serving, I hope to inspire each of you to recognize the immense power within yourselves. Divine light resides in all of us, waiting to be awakened.

The path ahead is not easy. Challenges will come, and shadows will rise. But I promise you this: with balance as our guide and unity as our strength, we will create a realm where all beings can thrive—in abundance, in peace, and in the light of eternal harmony.

Let us walk this path together, as one. For Etheria, for the realms, and for the balance of all that is.

Thank you."

As Aurora finished, a profound silence blanketed the hall. For a moment, no one moved, mesmerized by her words and the energy they carried. Then, as if on cue, the hall erupted in applause and cheers, the sound of unity and hope echoing through the Etherian skies.

As part of the celebration, Aurora received numerous gifts:

A celestial staff from Aetheria, symbolizing wisdom and guidance.

A gem of prophecy from the Queen of Luminor, allowing her glimpses into potential futures.

A cloak of invisibility from Zephyra, to move unseen when required.

A healing chalice from Aquarion, capable of mending even the gravest injuries.

An enchanted map of Etheria's hidden places from the Guardians of Knowledge.

Tessa, however, gave Aurora gifts of the heart. She presented her with **ancient scriptures** filled with Etheria's secrets and a precious book written by Aurora's mother, Elara. The book contained Elara's experiences, teachings, and hidden wisdom about Etheria and the mysteries of the universe.

"Your mother," Tessa said, her voice filled with emotion, "was not only a queen but also a visionary. Her writings will guide you in ways I cannot."

Aurora clutched the book close, feeling an overwhelming connection to her mother.

Chapter Eleven: Material and Spiritual Wealth: The Eternal Dance

That night, after the grand coronation and the heartfelt celebrations that followed, Aurora retired to her chamber in Etheria's palace. The room, adorned with soft hues of silver and gold, seemed to hum with the energy of the day's events. Exhausted yet fulfilled, Aurora sat by the window, gazing at the endless starlit sky. She felt a strange pull, an invitation to close her eyes and surrender to the dreamscape.

As soon as she drifted into sleep, a radiant vision unfolded. She found herself standing in a serene, boundless meadow bathed in golden light. The air was filled with the gentle hum of life, and a warm breeze carried the faint scent of flowers she couldn't name. Before her stood a magnificent gathering—her parents, Magnus and Elara, her ancestors, and countless others who carried the same regal yet serene aura.

Her father, King Magnus, stepped forward first. He looked as strong and noble as she remembered, yet his eyes carried a tenderness that pierced her heart.

"My daughter," he said, his voice deep and soothing, "you have risen to fulfil the destiny we always knew was yours. You embody the strength of our lineage, the wisdom of Etheria, and the light that will guide all realms."

Her mother, Elara, followed, her presence glowing like the moonlight. "Aurora, my precious child," she said with a voice as soft as a lullaby, "you have faced trials that many would crumble under, yet you have emerged radiant. I am so proud of the woman you've become. Remember, your happiness is the greatest gift you can give yourself and the world."

Aurora's ancestors, a magnificent lineage of kings, queens, warriors, scholars, and sages, surrounded her in a protective circle. One by one, they extended their blessings:

"May your wisdom guide the realms into harmony."

"May your strength inspire generations to come."

"May your heart remain open to love and joy, even amidst the challenges."

"May you never lose sight of the light within, even in the darkest times."

Aurora's eyes welled up with tears as she felt their collective energy wrap around her like a warm embrace. She knelt, overwhelmed by their love and support.

"But I miss you all," Aurora whispered. "Your guidance, your presence. It feels so heavy at times to bear this alone."

Elara stepped forward and knelt beside her. "You are never alone, my child. We are with you in every breath, every heartbeat, and every ray of light. Trust your path, and know that you are deeply loved."

Her father placed a hand on her shoulder. "Stay happy, Aurora. Joy is your true strength. It is the light that dispels the darkness."

The golden meadow shimmered, and the figures began to fade. Just before they disappeared, her ancestors spoke in unison, their voices like a celestial melody:

"Shine bright, Aurora. The realms need your light."

Aurora awoke with the first rays of dawn streaming into her chamber. Her heart felt full, and a renewed sense of purpose coursed through her. Though her parents and ancestors were not physically present, she felt their presence more profoundly than ever. Their blessings were with her, and their words echoed in her soul as a guiding force for the journey ahead.

She whispered into the morning light, "I will make you proud. I promise to stay happy, for myself, for Etheria, and for the balance of all realms."

Tessa took Aurora on a grand tour of Etheria. The vast empire was breathtaking, with its floating cities, crystal forests, glowing rivers, and energy fields pulsating with life. Every corner of Etheria held wonders Aurora had never imagined—temples dedicated to the elements, ancient libraries guarded by spiritual sentinels, and training grounds for Etheria's warriors.

Aurora marveled at the beauty but felt a void in her heart. She longed for Clara, Victor, and Elias, who had been her grounding force in her earthly life.

During a quiet moment in the palace gardens, Aurora approached Tessa with a question that had been weighing heavily on her heart. "Tessa, I have seen so much of Etheria today, yet it feels incomplete without Clara, Victor, and Elias. Where could Zalarak be hiding them? Where should I begin my search?"

Tessa's expression turned serious. "Zalarak's nature is to conceal his greatest secrets in the shadows. His lairs are always in the forgotten corners of realms, places where light rarely penetrates. You must start with the **Caverns of Obscura**, an ancient and perilous network of caves on the edge of Etheria. These caves are said to be a nexus of hidden dimensions, a place where one can hide anything— or anyone."

Aurora's determination solidified. She decided to begin her search immediately. She gathered her allies, including her trusted divine forces, and prepared for the journey into the Caverns of Obscura.

Before departing, Aurora addressed the Etherian Council. "Though I am now your queen, my first duty is to those who have given me unconditional love and support. I will bring Clara, Victor, and Elias back to Etheria, no matter the cost."

Aurora's resolve inspired the people of Etheria, who pledged their support. Tessa gave her another piece of advice: "Remember, Aurora, while light can penetrate the darkest corners, it must also remain vigilant. Zalarak thrives on distraction, and your focus is your greatest strength."

Aurora, armed with the gifts she had received, the wisdom of her mother's book, and the support of Etheria's forces, set out on her quest. As she ventured toward the unknown, the entire realm held its breath, praying for her success and waiting for their queen to return, triumphant once again.

Chapter Twelve: The Caverns of Obscura

Aurora's journey to find Clara, Victor, and Elias was relentless. Guided by Tessa's wisdom and her own unshakable determination, she ventured into the mysterious Caverns of Obscura. These ancient caves, perched on the edge of Etheria, were known as a labyrinth of hidden dimensions, a place where light barely reached and secrets remained buried.

As she entered the mouth of the cavern, a chilling wind wrapped around her, carrying whispers of forgotten souls. The air was dense with an energy that made even Aurora, now the Queen of Etheria, pause. She took a deep breath, her inner light pulsating as she summoned courage. "If Zalarak thinks shadows can hide the truth, he has underestimated me," she murmured.

Inside, the darkness was impenetrable. Aurora lit a torch with a snap of her fingers, its flame glowing with a mystical blue hue infused by her powers. She moved cautiously, the echoes of her footsteps bouncing eerily off the cavern walls. Each step felt like an intrusion into a realm untouched by time.

Aurora searched every corner, her senses sharp and attuned. After hours of navigating narrow passages and crossing treacherous ledges, she stumbled upon a hidden chamber. The sight froze her in place. Dozens of figures—men, women, and even children—were bound by ethereal chains, their faces pale and eyes hollow. They were prisoners of Zalarak, trapped by his dark influence.

Aurora's heart ached at the sight. "Who are you?" she asked gently, kneeling beside an elderly woman who looked too frail to speak.

"We are... forgotten," the woman rasped, tears streaming down her face. "Zalarak trapped us here. He feeds on our despair, our fear. We thought no one would come."

Aurora closed her eyes, her light intensifying as she reached into the depths of her power. "You're not forgotten anymore," she said firmly. Raising her hands, she channelled a surge of radiant energy that shattered the chains binding the prisoners. One by one, they gasped as their freedom was restored.

The freed captives knelt before Aurora, tears of gratitude streaming down their faces. "You are the light Etheria has awaited," they said in unison, their voices trembling with emotion.

But Aurora knew her mission wasn't over. These were not Clara, Victor, or Elias. The shadows still concealed her loved ones.

Returning to the surface with the rescued prisoners, Aurora found Tessa waiting, her expression grave. "Zalarak's cunning runs deeper than we imagined," Tessa said. "These people were a distraction, a test of your resolve. But your instincts were correct—his secrets are hidden in the darkest corners."

"Where should I go next?" Aurora asked, frustration flickering in her voice despite her calm demeanor.

Tessa's gaze turned inward, as if searching the infinite threads of the universe. "The Caverns of Obscura are only a gateway. Zalarak's true lair lies deeper, concealed within a forgotten dimension. You'll need to seek the Portal of Echoes, an ancient gateway within the caverns. It's a perilous path, but you must find it. Clara, Victor, and Elias are running out of time."

Aurora clenched her fists, her resolve hardening. "Then I will find the portal and uncover whatever Zalarak is hiding. He cannot keep them from me forever."

As the freed captives left, Aurora felt a surge of gratitude and hope radiating from them. Their blessings surrounded her like a protective shield, their voices echoing in her mind: "You are the light in the darkness, Aurora. Keep shining."

The cavern loomed behind her, its shadows deeper than ever, but Aurora's heart burned brighter with each passing moment. She knew the journey would be fraught with danger, yet she was determined. For Etheria, for her loved ones, and for every soul still trapped in Zalarak's shadow, Aurora vowed to keep fighting.

With Tessa's guidance and the light of Etheria within her, Aurora prepared to delve even deeper into the Caverns of Obscura, where the line between dimensions blurred and the ultimate battle awaited.

Aurora stood outside the Caverns of Obscura, her mind racing with possibilities. The captives she had freed had mentioned faint whispers about a hidden prison where Zalarak kept his most prized captives. Aurora turned to Tessa, who appeared beside her, her presence as calm and steady as a mountain.

"Zalarak's web is intricate," Tessa said, her eyes narrowing. *"But there is a place that fits this description—a hidden forest beyond the Shadow Veil, a place shielded by dark magic. It's a sanctuary for those he seeks to isolate completely."*

Aurora's breath hitched. The Shadow Veil was known to be treacherous, its air thick with illusions meant to disorient even the strongest minds. But there was no hesitation in her heart.

"Tell me how to get there," Aurora said, determination flaring in her eyes.

Tessa extended her hand, tracing a glowing map in the air. "Follow this path. Use the light within you to dispel the illusions. And, Aurora, trust your instincts. You are closer to them than you realize."

The journey through the Shadow Veil was harrowing. Aurora encountered mirages that tugged at her heart, illusions of Clara's laughter, Victor's comforting voice, and Elias's mischievous smile. But with each step, she centered herself in her light, banishing the shadows.

When she finally reached the hidden prison, it was empty. The air was stale, the faint scent of fear and despair lingering. Aurora's heart sank. "They were here," she whispered, kneeling to touch the ground.

The energy around her buzzed faintly, and she closed her eyes, focusing. Images flooded her mind—Clara, Victor, and Elias breaking free from their bonds, running through the dense forest, their faces lit with hope. But there was more. She saw Elias, bruised and bleeding, shielding Clara and Victor from a swarm of shadowy creatures.

"They're on the move," Aurora said aloud, rising to her feet.

Tessa's voice echoed in her mind. "Follow the wind, Aurora. Your bond with them will guide you."

Aurora moved swiftly through the dense forest, her senses sharpened by the urgency of her search. The faint trail of energy left by her loved ones was like a heartbeat, guiding her through the tangled maze of trees. The forest seemed alive, almost sentient—branches swayed to clear her path, while shadows flickered at the edge of her vision, both warning and watching. Her heart pounded in rhythm with the whispers that called to her, each step fueled by the hope of reunion.

Hours stretched like days as she pressed forward. Just when doubt began to creep in, a faint cry pierced the stillness. Her breath hitched, and without hesitation, she broke into a sprint, pushing through the forest's last barrier to reach the source.

In a clearing bathed in dim moonlight, the scene before her stole her breath. Clara and Victor were huddled together on the ground, their faces streaked with dirt and tears, their expressions shifting from fear to relief as their eyes met Aurora's. The bond of their love and longing was palpable, but it was Elias who caught Aurora's full attention.

He stood protectively in front of them, his body battered, his shirt torn and stained with blood. His makeshift weapon—a sturdy branch entwined with faintly glowing vines—quivered slightly in his grip, a testament to his exhaustion. Yet his stance remained firm, defiant against whatever dangers had threatened them.

Clara's voice cracked with emotion as she reached out. "Aurora… is it really you?" Tears streamed down her face, her relief overwhelming.

Elias turned to face Aurora, his eyes meeting hers with a mix of vulnerability and unyielding determination. His voice was raw but steady as he spoke. "I told them we'd find you. But they came for us before we could. I fought… as long as I could."

Aurora's heart broke at the sight of his injuries and the weight of his courage. She rushed to them, her hands already glowing with the familiar warmth of healing energy. Kneeling before Elias, she gently cupped his face, her touch soft but resolute. "You are so brave, Elias. You've protected them with everything you had," she said, her voice thick with emotion yet steady, a rock in the midst of the storm.

Elias faltered, the tension in his body releasing as the glow of her energy began to soothe his wounds. Clara and Victor moved closer, their hands clutching Aurora as though anchoring themselves to her presence. For a moment, the weight of the world lifted as they embraced, the years of separation dissolving into the intensity of this reunion.

This was no ordinary meeting; it was the convergence of unbreakable bonds, forged in love and resilience, reaffirmed by their shared struggles. The forest around them seemed to hold its breath, the moonlight casting a protective glow over the clearing as if the universe itself was bearing witness to their reunion.

Aurora placed her hands on Elias's wounds, her energy flowing into him. His breathing steadied, and the color returned to his face. "Thank you," he whispered, his voice barely audible.

She turned to Clara and Victor, embracing them tightly. "You're safe now," she said. "No one will harm you again."

Victor's voice broke as he spoke. "We knew you'd come, Aurora. We never stopped believing in you."

As the night deepened, Aurora set up a protective barrier around the clearing. They rested, her light keeping the darkness at bay. For the first time in years, she felt a sense of completeness, her loved ones back within her reach.

As they rested, Tessa's image appeared beside Aurora, her expression both proud and solemn. "Elias's bravery saved them," she said. "But the battle is far from over. Zalarak will not take this defeat lightly. He will strike again, and harder, if he gets a chance."

Aurora nodded, her resolve firm. "We'll be ready. Together, we're stronger than he realizes."

Tessa's eyes softened. "You've proven that light and love can triumph over the darkest forces. Rest tonight, Aurora. Tomorrow, the next chapter of your journey begins."

As the night deepened, Aurora held her loved ones close, the stars above shining brighter than ever. Her heart was full, but she knew the path ahead was still fraught with challenges. For now, though, she allowed herself to bask in the warmth of reunion, the light within her burning brighter than ever.

Aurora's return to her world marked a new chapter, not just for herself but for her family. The reunion with Clara, Victor, and Elias in Etheria had strengthened their bond, and now they were ready to explore life together in Aurora's dazzling yet demanding material world.

The mansion bustled with renewed energy as they settled in. Elias, still in awe of the city and Aurora's luxurious life, began his training under her guidance. Aurora introduced him to the art of meditation and the healing energies that flowed naturally within Etheria but required patience and practice in the human realm. Elias, though young and curious, showed remarkable focus, his bond with Aurora growing stronger with every session.

Aurora often found herself reminiscing about the simpler times when Clara had lovingly sung lullabies to her. One particular memory surfaced—Clara mentioning her dream of being a singer, a dream she had sacrificed to raise Aurora and lead a modest life in the countryside.

One crisp evening, lying under the vast open sky in the mansion's garden, Aurora rested her head on Clara's lap. The stars twinkled above like diamonds scattered across velvet, and the gentle breeze carried the faint scent of blooming flowers.

"Mom," Aurora said with a playful smile, "remember when you told me about your dream of becoming a singer and traveling the world?"

Clara laughed softly, her voice tinged with nostalgia. "Ah, those were the dreams of a girl who didn't know how life would unfold."

"Well," Aurora said, sitting up and looking into Clara's eyes, "that girl is about to make her dream come true. Starting tomorrow, your singing lessons begin."

Clara's laughter turned into surprise. "Aurora, what are you saying?"

Aurora grinned, her voice filled with mischief. "I've already arranged everything. Get ready to rediscover that voice of yours. The world is waiting to hear it."

Victor, overhearing the conversation, chuckled. "If Clara's learning to sing, I might as well join her. It's never too late, right?"

Aurora laughed along with them. "Absolutely not, Dad. Let's make it a family affair. You can learn music while I train Elias in meditation and healing."

With the household buzzing with new activities, Aurora found a quiet corner in her mansion to turn her attention to the gifts Tessa had bestowed upon her in Etheria. Among them was a collection of ancient scriptures, texts brimming with the wisdom of Etheria's energy system and universal laws.

But the book that caught Aurora's eye was the one written by her mother. Its cover was simple, yet it radiated a warmth that drew her in. As she opened it, the scent of old parchment filled the air, and the pages revealed the elegant handwriting of her mother.

The book began with heartfelt reflections:

"To my dear Aurora,

If you are reading this, it means you've grown into the extraordinary woman I always believed you would become. This is not just a book; it is a piece of me—a record of my experiences, my dreams, and the secrets I could never share with you in person."

Aurora's fingers lingered on the page as tears welled in her eyes. She read on, captivated by her mother's words. The book detailed Clara's journey—her love for music, her struggles as a young woman torn between her aspirations and the responsibilities that life thrust upon her, and her secret encounters with the mystical forces of Etheria.

One passage caught Aurora's attention:

"I knew from the moment I held you in my arms that you were destined for greatness, Aurora. You are the bridge between two worlds—the guardian of balance. Your journey will not be easy, but remember, the light within you is stronger than any shadow."

Aurora closed the book momentarily, her heart full of love and gratitude. She made a silent vow to honor her mother's legacy, not just by succeeding in her ventures but by living a life of balance, compassion, and purpose.

The next morning, the mansion came alive with the sound of Clara's voice as her singing lessons began. Victor, too, was enthusiastic about learning music, often teasing Clara about his progress. Meanwhile, Elias continued his meditation and healing sessions with Aurora, his confidence growing with every practice.

Aurora spent her days immersed in her business, her nights with her family, and her solitary hours delving into the scriptures. The mansion, once a symbol of material success, now became a sanctuary of growth, creativity, and spiritual awakening.

Aurora knew the road ahead would be filled with challenges, but with her family by her side and her mother's wisdom as her guide, she felt ready to face anything. Life, after all, was a perfect blend of dreams realized, lessons learned, and love shared—a melody that resonated across both worlds she called home.

The mansion was alive with purpose, its halls echoing with the laughter and ambition of a reunited family. Each member had found their path to growth, and the air was charged with possibility. One evening, as Aurora sat in her study reviewing her business reports, Elias approached her, a glimmer of curiosity and determination in his eyes.

"Aurora," Elias began hesitantly, *"I've been thinking. I love learning about healing and meditation, but... I also want to study science and computers. I've always been fascinated by how things work, and I want to understand more about the world around us."*

Aurora smiled warmly, her heart swelling with pride. "That's wonderful, Elias. Science and technology are powerful tools, and understanding them can open endless doors. Let's start by finding you a good teacher for your basic studies. If you show me dedication and do well, I'll help you get admission to the State University. How does that sound?"

Elias's face lit up with joy. "Really? You'd do that for me?"

"Of course," Aurora said, ruffling his hair affectionately. "You're family, Elias, and I want you to have every opportunity to chase your dreams."

Within days, Aurora had arranged for a tutor to visit the mansion and begin Elias's lessons. As she watched him delve into his studies with unbridled enthusiasm, she felt a deep sense of fulfillment. Each step Elias took toward his dreams was a testament to the power of guidance, love, and belief.

Late one night, after ensuring her family was asleep, Aurora retired to her private reading corner with her mother's book in hand. The flickering candlelight cast dancing shadows on the walls as she opened the cherished pages once more.

The book's tone shifted as it delved into the love story of her parents. Aurora learned about the magnetic connection between Clara and Victor—how they had met, the struggles they faced, and the deep, enduring love that had sustained them through hardships. Each word seemed to hum with emotion, painting vivid pictures of their tender moments and the strength they found in one another.

As Aurora read about her parents' love, a strange ache stirred in her chest. For the first time, she found herself yearning for a connection like theirs—one that could transcend boundaries and bring meaning to her journey.

Her thoughts wandered. What would it be like to share her life with someone who could understand her dual existence, her purpose, and her soul? Would there be someone out there who could complement her strengths, challenge her mind, and ignite her heart?

The question lingered as Aurora closed the book and gazed out of her window at the moonlit garden. Her heart, so long devoted to her mission and her family, now whispered a new desire: to find the love of her life.

In the chapters of her life yet to be written, Aurora knew this search would take her on a journey unlike any she had embarked upon before. It would challenge her in ways she couldn't yet imagine, leading her to new corners of the world and realms of her soul.

As she drifted into sleep, her dreams shimmered with visions of the future. Love awaited her—its light guiding her toward uncharted paths.

Coming Next (Volume -2): Aurora's Journey to Love

As Aurora stood amidst the radiant aftermath of her battle with Zalarak, a quiet determination settled in her heart. Though victorious, she knew this was only the beginning. The balance of the realms was fragile, and new challenges loomed on the horizon. Darkness, though subdued for now, would rise again. To protect the light and maintain harmony, Aurora would need to confront even greater forces, unlock deeper truths about herself, and strengthen her connection to the universal energies.

But as the dawn of a new journey approached, another realization stirred within her—a yearning she could no longer ignore. Aurora's path was not just about battles and realms; it was also about the mysteries of her own heart. Somewhere out there, her soulmate awaited—a connection prophesied yet obscured by destiny's veil.

In the next volume of *The Billionaire Mystic*, Aurora's story takes an exhilarating turn as she embarks on a quest not only to fortify the balance of the realms but also to discover the love of her life. Through serendipitous encounters, divine guidance, and moments of introspection, her journey will explore the profound interplay between destiny and desire.

Will Aurora find the one who complements her light, or will her search reveal that the love she seeks has always resided within herself? Stay tuned for an epic tale of courage, passion, and the unyielding power of the human spirit.

Life Lessons from Aurora's Journey

Aurora's story is a testament to the transformative power of faith, resilience, and self-discovery. Her path, marked by challenges and triumphs, mirrors lessons that guide us in our own lives:

1. **Inner Strength Through Faith**
   Aurora's unwavering belief in her purpose reflects the profound truth found in sacred texts like the *Hanuman Chalisa* and *Sunderkand*. These are more than hymns; they are roadmaps to resilience. They remind us that faith is a source of infinite strength, guiding us through darkness and helping us face life's trials with clarity and confidence.

2. **Turning Challenges into Opportunities**
   Just as Hanuman Ji leapt across the ocean and moved mountains in service of Lord Ram, Aurora transformed her adversities into stepping stones for growth. Her battles taught her—and us—that every challenge hides an opportunity to evolve, adapt, and emerge stronger. Obstacles aren't barriers; they are invitations to tap into our courage and creativity.

3. **Self-Realization Unlocks Infinite Potential**
   Aurora's greatest weapon wasn't external power but her inner light—the strength she discovered through introspection and spiritual practices. Her journey underscores the importance of exploring the inner self, where untapped potential lies dormant. Self-realization isn't just a goal; it's a lifelong journey to awaken the divine spark within, unlocking possibilities we never imagined.

Aurora's experiences remind us that life's greatest battles are often within, and the most profound victories come from embracing our true essence. In her story, we find inspiration to rise, to seek, and to shine brighter than ever before.

Inspirational Exercises and Questions

1.   Reflect on a moment when you faced a seemingly insurmountable challenge. How did you overcome it? What inner strength did you tap into?

2.   Spend five minutes each morning visualizing your highest self—how you look, act, and feel when you are in complete harmony with your goals and purpose.

3.   Write down three ways you can incorporate devotion or meditation into your daily routine.

4.   Ask yourself: What is one fear or limiting belief holding me back from my full potential? How can I take the first step to confront it?

5.   Chant a mantra or affirmation daily for a week. Observe how your thoughts, energy, and attitude shift.

Daily Routine to transform your life

- Chant the Hanuman Chalisa 11 times daily.

- Recite the Sunderkand from Ram Charit Manas every day.

- Meditate for an hour, focusing on your breath and divine connection.

- Fast every Monday to elevate your spiritual energy and discipline.

- Do Surya Namaskar (Sun Salutation) or Yoga every day to be aligned.

This practice has been the author's steadfast companion for 11 years and serves as a pillar of strength and clarity.

Powerful Ram Mantras:

1. **"Om   Shri   Ramaya   Namah"**
A mantra to invoke Lord Ram's divine blessings and protection. It brings strength, peace, and spiritual clarity.

2. **"Shri Ram Chandra Kripalu Bhajman Haran Bhav   Bhaya   Darunam"**
This mantra praises Lord Ram's compassion and grace, helping to remove fear and negativity.

3. **"Ram Rameti Rameti Rame Raame Manorame, Sahasranama   Tattulyam   Rama   Nama Varanane"**
This mantra, said to hold the power of chanting Lord Vishnu's thousand names, is deeply calming and spiritually uplifting.

4. **"Jai   Shri   Ram"**
A simple yet powerful chant that invokes courage, devotion, and divine strength in every moment.

5. **"Ram   Bhakta   Hanuman   Ki   Jai"**
This chant connects the energy of Lord Ram and Hanuman, bringing protection and the resolve to face life's challenges.

6. **"Sita   Ram   Sita   Ram"**
This mantra celebrates the divine union of Lord Ram and Goddess Sita, symbolizing harmony, devotion, and spiritual balance.

7. **"Ram   Raksha   Stotra   Mantra"**
"Charitam   Raghunathasya   Shatakoti Pravistaram,   Ekaikamaksharam   Pumsam

Mahapatakanashanam."
This mantra is part of the *Ram Raksha Stotra*, offering protection and liberation from negativity.

Chant these mantras with devotion and intention to invite the energy of Lord Ram into your life.

Call to Action

Your journey toward balance, growth, and self-realization begins now. Take the first step by exploring your inner potential and embracing the practices that resonate with your soul.

•	Connect with Divine Guidance to access workshops, consultations, and personalized life strategies.

•	Visit our website (**Divineguidanceastrology.com**) or follow us on social media to stay inspired and informed.

Email ID: divineguidance3355@gmail.com

IG: @DIVINEGUIDANCE333555

Facebook: Angelguidance

•	Share your experiences and stories with us; we'd love to hear how The Billionaire Mystic has impacted your life.

Endnote / Closing Reflection

As you close the final page of this book, remember that your journey doesn't end here—it is only the beginning. Every step you take toward aligning your material goals with your spiritual essence brings you closer to your highest self.

The universe is abundant, and you are a divine part of its infinite possibilities. Keep striving, keep believing, and most importantly, keep turning inward for the answers.

May your path be filled with light, strength, and grace.

With love and blessings,

Shalini Pathak

NOTE

NOTE

9 798889 673182